CHARLIE'S WEB

A Mystery

by

L. L. Thrasher

A Write Way Publishing Book

This is a work of fiction. Names, characters, locales and incidents are either the product of the author's imagination or are used fictitiously, and any resemblance to actual persons, living or dead, is entirely coincidental.

Write Way Publishing
PO Box 441278
Aurora, CO 80044

First Edition: 2000

ISBN 1-885173-66-0

1 2 3 4 5 6 7 8 9

For my friend
Julianne Kloc Trychta

With special thanks to
Carol Babel
for sending me a newspaper clipping
about a billboard
and to
Detective Steve Baty
for answering all my "cop questions."

CHAPTER ONE

Jonathan was panting right into my ear, so when I felt a funny tingle all over my body, I thought it was just a reaction to that. The feeling was so strange though that I opened my eyes—and someone was standing by the bed!

I screamed, but I was a little breathless, so it sounded more like a shuddery shriek. Jonathan misinterpreted it completely. He was so inspired I had to put my hands over my head and press them against the headboard to keep him from driving my head right through it.

"Sorry. Bad timing." A man's voice, familiar, almost like . . .

"Jonathan—"

"Yeah, baby," he muttered.

"Jonathan!"

"Oh, *yeah,*" he said, and my hands slipped and my head banged against the headboard twice and he collapsed on me.

I lifted my head to look past his shoulders. "Jonathan, someone's—" But there was no one by the bed. I craned my neck, trying to see the floor at the side of the bed. Had he really been there? He couldn't have really been there. But I'd seen him, not his features, just the shape of a man, tall and broad-shouldered and . . . something about his hair. What about his hair? I couldn't quite remember. He'd been only a shadow lit from behind by the moonlight. He had seemed so real though. And he spoke. I heard him speak. His voice was familiar, almost like . . . I couldn't quite remember.

"What?" Jonathan sounded sleepy.

"Nothing."

"Someone what?"

"*Noth*ing, Jonathan."

He did a couple push-ups, biceps bulging and shoulder muscles bunching. Jonathan's got a great body. "That was fun. You want to do it again?"

"Not right now."

He laughed breathlessly. "I didn't mean right this minute." He rolled off and stretched out at my side and began stroking various parts of my body. "You mean you wouldn't want to do it again right now? Assuming, of course, that I could–"

"Did you hear something? Someone talking?"

"When?"

"Just a minute ago."

"A bomb could have gone off under the bed a minute ago and I wouldn't have noticed. What do you mean, someone talking? Outside?"

"Um, no. Not exactly. You didn't hear anything? A voice?"

"No. Did you?"

"I'm not sure."

"You must've imagined it. I didn't hear anything."

"Don't do that. I'm trying to think."

"You can't think while I'm doing this? Interesting. How about if I do this?"

I rolled away from him and got out of bed, stooping to pick up my pale blue terry cloth robe from the floor. I slipped it on, cinching the sash tight.

Jonathan sat up cross-legged on the bed, the sheet all in a tangle around him. "What's wrong, Lizbet? Something I did? Something I didn't do? Something I did but didn't do right or didn't do enough of or did too much of? The secret to good sex is communication. I read that somewhere. Or maybe it was the secret to good communication is sex. Come back to bed. Let's communicate some more. We can talk all night."

I was looking around the room, which wasn't really dark at all, what with the drapes being open so only sheer curtains covered the sliding glass door to the balcony, letting in the light from the full moon. Full moon. *Werewolves!* I told myself to stop being silly. But I'd seen . . . something. Maybe it had been a trick of light and shadow. But he had seemed so real. And I heard him speak. I shivered, hugging myself and bowing my head. Maybe I was going crazy.

Jonathan got off the bed and put his arms around me, squeezing me against him for a second, my folded arms between us, then he leaned back to look down at my face. "What's wrong? You're scaring the hell out of me."

"It isn't you. Nothing's wrong. I just . . ."

I just thought I saw . . . a ghost.

A ghost.

I felt something in my mind, a sliding feeling, like a bit of memory slipping into place. A *ghost.* Of course. I'd had a ghost before. Charlie. Charlie Bilbo, Jonathan's father. Jonathan's father, whose voice was very much like his son's. How could I have forgotten? I remembered now, just like it was yesterday, only it was really six months ago, in April, when a skeleton was dug up by the men who were putting in my swimming pool and Charlie appeared to me. I'd helped solve his murder, which happened back in 1969.

I remembered Charlie now, Charlie with his bright blue eyes and long blond hair–long hair, that was it, he had long hair–and hippie clothes, a silver and turquoise peace symbol on his chest. How could I have forgotten Charlie? How could I possibly forget about a ghost? I shivered again and felt Jonathan's arms tighten around me. How could I seriously think I'd known a ghost? Maybe I *was* going crazy.

"Lizbet?"

"Everything's okay, Jonathan. I just . . ." The truth was impossible to tell so I lied instead: "I suddenly thought about Duke and Lady. I was just feeling sad, I guess." Duke and Lady were my parents. They died a few years ago from carbon monoxide poisoning in their trailer. Jonathan gently took my wrists and uncrossed my arms then pressed my body against his again and rubbed my back and nuzzled my neck. He understands about parents. His father–Charlie, my ghost Charlie, I *did* have a ghost, Charlie was really here, I remember him being here–Charlie died when Jonathan was just a toddler. But Jonathan believed his father ran off. He didn't know Charlie was dead until after the bones turned up in my backyard. And then Jonathan's mother disappeared and hasn't been seen since. Jonathan knows all about parents and how they make you feel.

He suddenly scooped me up in his arms and kissed me, soft little feathery kisses darting all around my lips. I put my arms tight around his neck. "I don't want any ghosts, Jonathan." My voice came out thick, full of tears.

"Shhh," he said, "shhh," and put me down on the bed. He untied my robe and slid his body against mine. He felt warm and solid and real. "No ghosts," he said.

He meant memories, not real ghosts, but it helped anyway and after a while–after I stopped wondering if Charlie was really real and after I stopped wondering why he had come back and after I stopped worrying about him watching us and after I stopped wondering if I really was going crazy because why else would I be worrying about a ghost?—after all that, I finally stopped thinking about ghosts and pretty soon I stopped thinking about anything, but every once in a while I opened my eyes, just to check. There was no one standing by the bed.

Chapter Two

He didn't come back until dawn. The tingle woke me. I'd been expecting it. I knew he would be back, because before I went to sleep I thought about it some more and I knew it was true. Charlie was a ghost and he'd been here in April and I'd seen him and talked to him. And now he was back. I had *very* mixed feelings about that. Charlie almost got me killed in April.

"Hello, Lizbet," he said. Those were the first words he'd ever said to me, back in April.

I put a finger to my lips, which was kind of silly because he could have shouted and no one else would have heard him. I leaned over and whispered in Jonathan's ear, telling him I was just getting up for a minute. He mumbled something and thumped a fist into his pillow then snuggled his face into it. I had put on a long blue cotton nightgown when we finally decided to use the bed for sleeping. I slipped my robe over it and tiptoed out of the bedroom.

I went downstairs to the casual living room, which is all done in soft greens and blues and is my favorite room in the house, except for my bedroom when Jonathan is here. Yes, I also have a formal living room. I'm stinking rich, but only because my ex-husband, Tom Lange, struck it rich, then died and left everything to me. I'm just a little out of my element because before Tom died I was a waitress at a truck stop. I'm also a high school dropout with a police record. Only a juvenile record, though. Strictly minor stuff. No pun intended. Well, actually it was. I don't know why people always say "no pun intended" when you know they had to intend it because if they hadn't they most likely wouldn't even realize it was a pun, right?

I hadn't looked back to see if Charlie was following me. I knew he was because he needed a link to pass from one universe to another. Parallel universes, that's how he explained it to me in April. Charlie needed a link and I was it and he couldn't get too far away from me or he'd lose contact with my universe. Exactly what *Charlie's* universe is like is something he never explained and I never asked because I was never too sure I wanted to know anyway.

I sat down on the couch, curling my legs beneath me, and said, *"I'm mad at you,"* only I didn't say it out loud, I only thought it. Charlie had always claimed he couldn't read my mind unless I was deliberately trying to communicate with him, but I didn't completely believe that. Either he could read my mind whenever he wanted or he was extremely perceptive. Or I'm extremely transparent.

"Good, that means you remember everything now."

"Yeah, it all came back, just like a door opened or something."

"I see you and Jonathan hit it off."

I blushed, remembering the position I'd been in when he first arrived. *"You really should learn to knock."*

Charlie laughed, a great laugh, full of joy. Jonathan laughs the same way, but not often enough. They look alike, too. Jonathan's hair is a darker blond than Charlie's and clipped short, but otherwise they're very much the same. Charlie died when he was twenty-seven and hasn't changed a bit since. Jonathan is a little older than his father, which is only confusing if you think about it too much.

"Why are you here?"

"I need your help again."

"No, Charlie. Absolutely N-O, *no*. I'm not doing anything for you. In case you've forgotten—or maybe you don't know since you were already gone, but I almost got shot right out in front of the house."

"It worked out all right in the end, didn't it?"

"Yeah, I guess. Your name was cleared, did you know that? It was in the paper, all about how you were some kind of big hero."

"I thought it might turn out like that. Is Jonathan a deep sleeper?"

"Why?"

"You're talking out loud."

"Oh. Sorry." I pressed my lips together to remind myself to keep my mouth closed and said in my head, *"The bedroom's clear at the other end of the house. There's no way he could hear me."*

"I was worrying more about him noticing you're gone and coming downstairs looking for you. This house is too well-built to have creaky floors and the carpet's so thick you'd never hear anyone coming."

"All right, I'll try to remember. Anyway, the thing is, I can't have any kind of a normal life with you around. Doesn't it bother you that the truth never really came out? No one but me knows what really happened when you died, and I only remember it now that you're here. Doesn't that bother you?"

"Not really. Who's it hurting?"

I thought about that for a moment. Actually, it wasn't hurting anyone. Jonathan was a lot better off not knowing the whole truth about his father's murder. I'm not really the only one who knows what happened in 1969. Jonathan's mother knows but she'd never tell even if she did show up again, and the guy who murdered Charlie knows but he's in prison for the rest of his life and nobody would believe him if he did tell.

"I guess it isn't hurting anyone, but that really isn't the point. The point is that I'm not doing anything else for you. I can't*, Charlie. For pete's sake, people thought I was nuts the last time you were here. I just can't have a ghost popping into my life every few months. It isn't* normal.*"*

"It's not anything complicated, we just have to—"

"No. Absolutely, positively, one hundred percent *no!*"

"Who the hell are you talking to?"

Oh, *shit!* Jonathan was in the doorway, wearing navy blue boxer shorts and nothing else and looking positively gorgeous and a little sleepy and a whole lot confused.

"Nobody. I was talking to myself."

"No you weren't."

"Yes I was. Who on earth would I be talking to? There's no one here."

"I know what you sound like when you're talking to yourself and that wasn't it." Jonathan had walked a few feet into the room and was looking all around.

"Jeez, Jonathan. Okay, you caught me. It was my other boyfriend. Why don't you look under the couch? He's real skinny."

Oh, god, he looked so hurt, like a puppy when you yell at it. "Don't, Lizbet. Don't . . . I wasn't accusing you of anything. I just . . . I'm half asleep, I guess. I thought you were talking to someone."

Sometimes I'm a real jerk. I hurried across the room and put my arms around him and rested my cheek against his shoulder. He didn't put his arms around me, or even move. "I was . . . I got in an argument with a sales clerk the other day and she was real snooty and I was, well, my usual trashy self, and she made me look like an idiot and I was thinking about it and I was . . . I guess I was sort of pretending I was back at the store telling her off. I was embarrassed when I realized you'd heard me." I was actually crying a little. I'm such a good liar, I believe myself. His arms went around me in a tight hug for a moment and then he put his hands on my waist and gently pushed me back so he could look at my face.

"You're not trashy, honey. You shouldn't let things like that get to you." He stroked my hair back from my face and kissed me on the nose.

Men are so easy.

"Come back to bed," he said. "I missed you."

"Um . . ."

"Go on," Charlie said from somewhere behind me. *"I'll come back later. And Lizbet, you have to help me. Someone's life depends on it."*

I didn't look at Charlie but as I left the room, I thought, *"Nothing complicated, huh, Charlie? I haven't forgotten that I can send you away, so just leave me alone, okay?"* He didn't say anything and I wasn't even sure he was still there. We went back to bed. Jonathan went to sleep. I stared at the ceiling for a long time with my teeth clenched and butterflies fluttering in my stomach. Ghosts can be a real pain in the ass, you know?

CHAPTER THREE

"Have you seen the billboard?" Charlie asked, and my stomach did a horrible flip-flop. I'd seen hundreds of billboards but there was only one he could mean.

I was sitting cross-legged on my bed, which was covered with a white goose-down comforter enclosed in a pale blue duvet with eyelet trim. Duvet is pronounced *doo-vay*. I know because the woman at the store where I bought it told me so. She was so snooty she didn't even laugh when I said "doo-vette," she just corrected me in a whisper, like she wanted to be sure nobody noticed that she was being forced to wait on a total ignoramus. A duvet is like a great big pillowcase that you put over really expensive white goose-down comforters that are so soft and light you almost can't feel them.

Charlie was standing by the foot of the bed. It was about one-thirty and Jonathan had left a few minutes earlier. He didn't have to be at work until three, but he had to go to the dry cleaners to pick up his uniforms and then he was going to stop by his apartment in San Jose before going to work. He's a cop, but I like him anyway.

"Well?"

"Of course I've seen it . . . But that can't have anything to do with you, Charlie. She was killed . . . when? In nineteen seventy-three, wasn't it? You'd been dead for years by then." I did some quick math, writing the numbers on the duvet with my index finger. "She was only six years old when you died."

"It doesn't have anything to do with me. But it's not going to turn out right if we don't do something."

I frowned. "I don't get it, Charlie. I mean, it almost makes sense—you coming back to solve your own murder, but someone else's? What are you, some kind of vigilante ghost? Is this your punishment? You have to spend eternity solving old murders?"

"Not exactly. At least, I don't think so. I can't explain it, Lizbet. I don't understand it all myself. I only know that I'm back, and you're my link, and we have to do something or that girl's killer will never be caught and innocent people might get hurt."

"God, Charlie. Why *me?"*

"You're my link."

"Well, can't you pick another one?"

"I guess not." He sounded a little disappointed, like maybe I wasn't exactly his first choice.

"Hey, I did all right last time."

Charlie smiled. He has this absolutely glorious smile that takes your breath away and makes you hope the smile's for you. Just like Jonathan's smile, sometimes. *"You did fine. So you'll help me then?"*

"Not if I have a choice. Look, last time even after you went away I was still stuck with it. I had cops mad at me and men with guns coming after me . . . Jeez, Charlie, I don't want to go through that again."

"I don't think it'll be anything like that."

"But you don't know, do you? That's the problem: You'll get me into something and I'll end up having to get myself out.

It's a murder case, *unsolved*, which means the murderer is still out there somewhere. The cops must think he's still around, too, otherwise why would they bother with the billboard?"

"They don't know who killed her. They hope the billboard will jog someone's memory, or make someone who knows something feel guilty enough to finally step forward. Maybe you could offer a reward. You have plenty of money; maybe a reward would encourage someone to come forward."

"It's been over twenty-five years. If someone knew something why would they wait until now?"

"Protecting someone, or because they're afraid of the killer, or maybe they were just afraid of getting involved back then. The cops never believed that a little girl could be snatched off the street and her body hidden for three days before it was dumped off without someone knowing something about it. Maybe there's someone out there who always wondered about a friend or relative—or just an acquaintance—who was behaving suspiciously. Maybe they didn't know anything definite so they didn't come forward, thinking it was just unfounded suspicion and they didn't want to sic the cops on an innocent person by mistake. Maybe it was someone young and they're older now and talking to the cops won't be as frightening. All the cops need is a lead, then maybe they can break the case. The billboard makes it news again, forces people to think about it. Maybe someone has kept a guilty secret long enough."

"We aren't talking about repressed memories, are we? I read all about that in . . . a magazine. It sounded pretty hokey to me."

Charlie smiled. I think he suspected I really read all about it in a tabloid newspaper, which is true but I try to keep my secret vices secret, you know what I mean?

"I don't think it's anything like that. I just meant that someone who wasn't willing to talk in nineteen seventy-three might not feel as strong about it now. A lot of time has passed, they've gone on with their life, they've grown up; or maybe it wasn't a young person, maybe

it's someone who's getting up in years, maybe it's not a secret they want to take to their grave."

Charlie had taken his secret to the grave, not by choice really since he didn't expect to be murdered. But then he came back to haunt me. I wondered if he was going to keep coming back. What if I was stuck with him my whole life? Good grief, I didn't want a ghost pestering me for the rest of my life. It's really hard to act normal when someone no one else can see is tagging along with you everywhere you go, talking to you, making you do weird things you can't explain.

Charlie said, *"Her younger sister is married now and just had a baby. She would have children of her own, most likely. If someone hadn't killed her."* He was looking at me steadily, blue eyes wide open, trying to make me feel guilty. Well, I wasn't going to. Maybe he read my mind because he said, *"Why won't you help me, Lizbet?"*

I didn't answer, but I knew the reason: I didn't ever again want to be on my knees with a man pointing a gun at my head. I mean, nobody would want to go through that, right? I had bad dreams about it for weeks afterward, months really because sometimes I still dream about it, I still wake up in the night all clammy and hot and cold at the same time, remembering a man saying *Shoot her.* The fear, that's mostly what I dream about, being scared, scared of dying the way I was scared of dying in April, scared almost to death that a gunshot would be the last sound I'd ever hear. Maybe Charlie would have understood because a gunshot was the last thing he heard before he died, but I didn't really feel like talking about it.

He was still watching me, his right hand fiddling with the peace symbol that hung around his neck. Five turquoises were evenly spaced around the silver circle with the rocketship shape inside it. Charlie was wearing the clothes he died in: bellbottom jeans and leather sandals, a blue chambray workshirt and a fringed leather vest. The leather thong across his forehead was tied at the back of his head. He was working on a big undercover assignment when he was murdered. *"Okay,"* he said and I said, "Okay? That's it? Just, okay?"

"I can't force you to do something you aren't willing to do."

You coulda fooled me. I did lots of things I didn't want to do last time he was here. And didn't he just say *Innocent people might get hurt?* And didn't he say something earlier like *Someone's life might depend on it? Nothing dangerous.* Yeah, *right.*

"No, Charlie," I said, and he said, *"Goodbye, Lizbet,"* and he was gone, just like that. No more Charlie.

I should have felt relieved. Instead I felt sad, sort of the way I feel when I suddenly think about Duke and Lady, even after all these years. The house felt empty. Well, it *was* pretty much empty; no one was there but me, all by myself in a house with seven bathrooms. Eight really, because there's one in the studio apartment over the garage, where the housekeeper or cook would live if I had one, which I don't. I suddenly wished Jonathan was with me. I thought about calling him. Maybe I could catch him at his apartment. I leaned over toward the side of the bed, rolling awkwardly on my backside because I still had my legs crossed, and picked up the phone from the night stand. But I put it down again right away. I couldn't tell Jonathan about Charlie, I couldn't explain why I suddenly had this empty, lonely feeling, like I'd lost someone, like someone had died.

I had a horrible suspicion that when Charlie died he went to Cop Heaven, where eternity is just one big homicide investigation after another. The cops I know—Jonathan and his friends on the San Jose police force and John Sterling, who's the police chief here in Oak Valley—they all get really intense about big cases and can't think about anything else. Jonathan's a uniformed cop but he's always getting loaned to the detective division—the Bureau of Investigations, they call it in San Jose—when they need extra help and he's sure to make detective one of these days. When he's involved in an important case he'll suddenly stop kissing me to say something like, "His alibi checks out but I know the bastard's lying." *Real* romantic.

Maybe Charlie doesn't *have* to spend eternity solving murders, maybe he *gets* to, you know what I mean? Maybe that's what he wants to do most, so that's what he gets to do. If that's true, I wonder what I'll spend eternity doing. There isn't anything I do that's as important to me as being a cop is to the cops I know. I mean, I don't really want to spend eternity shopping for clothes, you know?

I uncrossed my legs and lay back on the bed, flat on my back, thinking about the billboard and wondering just what had happened back in 1973. It seemed funny that in all these years no one had figured it out. Not one person had ever come forward with information. The cops never had a single clue, not one good suspect. I rolled over and picked up the phone again, thinking I'd call Jonathan and see what he knew about the case. I pressed three numbers, then hung up. There was no way I could explain to Jonathan why I was suddenly dying of curiosity about the murder of Rachel Wright.

Dying of curiosity. I felt myself shiver.

CHAPTER FOUR

I don't remember 1973, of course—I'm only twenty-four—but I know all about it. History was Duke's favorite thing and he used to ramble on and on about things that happened in the past. By the time I was old enough to pay attention to him, Lady was sick to death of listening, so for most of my childhood I kept him company in the evenings out on the back porch, where he'd tilt an old kitchen chair back against the wall and prop his feet up on an overturned paint can and roll a fat marijuana cigarette.

Nineteen seventy-three, he says—or 1929 or 1969 or 1950 or 1861, it didn't matter, he knew all about just about any year—*Nineteen seventy-three; that was the year of Watergate, Lizzie-Lou, the year the shit really hit the fan.* He glances at Lady, who has a prissy look on her face like she would never say "shit" herself even though I've heard her say it plenty of times.

June seventeen, nineteen-seventy-two. That was when—

*Nineteen-seventy-*three, I say and he laughs and says, *This is background, you gotta understand the background,* the context, *you know what I mean, Lizzie-m'Lou? June seventeen, nineteen-seventy-two's when they broke into the Watergate Hotel for the second time; first time was earlier that year, in May, but they didn't get caught the first time, they got caught the second time and got arrested, a guy named James McCord and a bunch of Cubans, got caught red-handed.*

What'd they steal, Duke?

Didn't steal anything. It wasn't that kind of burglary. They were bugging the place and taking pictures of papers. Snooping.

Burglars steal TVs.

Not this kind of burglar, this kind is even worse. They were stealing information, Lizzie-bet, and information's the most important thing there is.

Why, Duke?

Because you can use information to make things happen the way you want them to, he says, taking a hit off his joint and lifting his chin to blow the smoke slowly upward. *They were in an office that belonged to the Democratic National Committee. Tricky Dick and his Republican buddies were snooping on the Democrats, wanting to make sure Nixon got re-elected that fall, which he did. 'Seventy-three's when Watergate blew wide open. Right after Nixon got inaugurated for his second term, James McCord squealed, told people he lied about Watergate because John Dean told him to. Dean was one of Nixon's White House lawyers. The Senate appointed a special prosecutor—Archibald Cox, the guy's name was—and then 'long about October Nixon ordered his Attorney-General to fire Cox but he quit instead of doing what Nixon wanted, and a couple guys under him quit, too. The Saturday Night Massacre, they called it. Cox got canned later on but it didn't do Nixon any good because the Senate was doing its own investigating. Agnew quit in October of 'seventy-three, too. Nixon's vice-president, Spiro Agnew. Stupid damn name, isn't it? He was charged with tax evasion, cheated on his taxes back when he was governor of Maryland. Had to resign in disgrace from the second highest office in the nation.*

Lady is standing in the kitchen, looking at us through the patched screen door. *Other things happened in 'seventy-three,* she says. *Roe versus Wade, that was in 'seventy-three. That's the Supreme Court decision that gave women the right to make decisions about their own bodies, Lizbet.*

Duke mutters something I don't quite catch, something about murder, and Lady turns and walks away, her back rigid.

Yeah, other things happened, Duke says, staring at the screen door where Lady is no longer standing. *All the usual shit happened. Jack Lemmon got the Academy Award for Best Actor for* Save the Tiger *and Glenda Jackson got Best Actress for* A Touch of Class. *Chick flicks, both of them. Best Picture went to* The Sting, *though. Now that was a movie. Robert Redford and Paul Newman, like in* Butch Cassidy and the Sundance Kid, *you know that movie, Lizzie-Lou?*

I shake my head and Duke sighs. I wish Lady would come back and listen to him so I don't have to. But I can't leave him all alone with no one to talk to.

The Exorcist *came out that year, too,* he says. *Scary movie, had a little girl in it whose head spun around in a circle.*

I spin around in a circle, my whole body, not just my head, but Duke isn't watching and it makes me dizzy so I stop. *Did they go to jail?* I ask. *That guy and the Cubans?*

Instead of answering he says, *It was all politics, you know what I mean?*

I don't, but I nod my head yes anyway, because if I say no he'll explain it to me. He explains it anyway.

A lot of things were going on in Washington in the fall of 1973, but in Oak Valley, California, which was a lot smaller then than it is now, Rachel Wright was bigger news than the Saturday Night Massacre.

Rachel Wright disappeared on Halloween, and the holiday wasn't the same in Oak Valley for years afterward. Some kids still went trick-or-treating but only with their parents and only before dark. Most kids went to Halloween parties at schools or churches. No one trick-or-treated after dark except for kids who were too old to be spooked by the story of Rachel Wright. At least, they were too old to let on that they were spooked.

Years after it happened, I heard all about Rachel Wright in Gilroy where I grew up. It's only about fifty miles from Oak Valley. Every Halloween, Lady told me about Rachel Wright and I was too scared to leave the house after dark, even when I was old enough to know that whoever snatched Rachel Wright wasn't likely to be in Gilroy, lurking in the shadows, looking for another little girl in a ghost costume made from a sheet. Rachel Wright scared me more than all those stories about razor blades in apples.

I never went trick-or-treating after dark until I was sixteen, the fall I dropped out of high school. I was way too old for trick-or-treating and so were the kids I was with. We were looking for kicks, looking for people who would tell us we were too old and refuse to give us candy so we could sneak back in the dead of night to throw eggs at their cars and toilet paper their houses. We stayed out until two in the morning, although we stopped ringing doorbells long before that because someone called the cops on us and they were cruising all around the neighborhood, looking for the troublemakers. We hid in the shadows in a vacant lot, talking dirty and drinking beer. When I got home Lady met me at the door and said, "Your father is going to kill you."

But Duke was already asleep, the cans from his last six-pack lined up on the coffee table—dead soldiers, he called them— and I didn't see him for a long time after that because I went to my room and stuffed some clothes in my backpack and ran away from home to live with a nineteen-year-old dropout who had a cute smile and made me shiver when he kissed me. He worked at a convenience store until he got caught stealing from the cash register. The night he was arrested I stuffed the same clothes in my backpack and ran away again, all the way to San Jose, which isn't very far from Gilroy but is a whole lot bigger. I stayed with a girl I knew and hung around the campus at San Jose State until I found another guy to live with. I was always good at finding guys to live with. But they were all stupid jerks, even the ones who were in college, and I always ended up waiting tables to buy their beer or make their bail.

Rachel Wright died before she was old enough to do stupid things on Halloween night, but she probably wouldn't have anyway. She was a straight-A student who had skipped a grade, so she was only ten, a year younger than most of the other kids in her sixth-grade class. Lady told me the teachers all cried at her funeral. I made a teacher mad enough to cry once, but I don't think any of them would have shown up at my funeral, unless maybe they felt like dancing.

Sometimes I wish I'd been more like Rachel Wright. Of course, if I had been I would never have married a sixty-two-year-old man when I was twenty-one, and I wouldn't have all his money now. And his house, and his cars, and his boat, and his stockbroker and accountant and lawyer. On the other hand, I wouldn't be taking a class so I could pass a high school equivalency test either, which was what I should have been thinking about instead of lying on my bed wondering what happened to poor Rachel Wright. I rolled off the bed and headed downstairs to gather up my study materials, as the teacher calls all the photocopied papers he seems to think I'm actually going read.

CHAPTER FIVE

Jonathan, whose last name is Dillon, not Bilbo, because when his mother divorced Charlie she took back her maiden name and changed Jonathan's name, too, not knowing her husband was dead—Jonathan told me back in August that I should get a GED, a General Education Development certificate, what Lady always called a dropout diploma. Right then, pleasing Jonathan seemed important—this was a few days after we started dating—so I signed up for a class that started in September, although I wondered if I couldn't just give a bunch of money to Oak Valley College and ask them for an honorary degree that I could hang on my wall so everyone would think I went to college.

"You can't buy everything, Lizbet" is what Jonathan said to that. He was right, I guess. I can't really buy an education and I can't buy a new past and I can't use my money to erase all the stupid things I've done and I can't pay off the sandman to stop bringing me those bad dreams. Besides, nobody would believe I went to college. I don't even know what *Macbeth* is about except that Lady Macbeth couldn't get the blood off her hands. I bought the *Cliff's Notes* one day when I was in a bookstore but I haven't read them yet. They're longer than the play.

My class is at the high school, Oak Valley High, not Gilroy High where I went until I dropped out, but it's still a high school and smells like gym shoes and hormones and I have to walk down a long echoing hall lined with lockers to get to the class.

The GED class meets twice a week at three in the afternoon. There's also an evening class but I signed up for the afternoon one because going to school in the evening just sounded awful. A lot of women with children are in the afternoon class because babysitting is provided. A couple high school girls with rings in their noses and eyebrows—and probably bellybuttons and who knows where else—watch the children in a room that has a connecting door into our classroom. The kids whine a lot, and the mothers keep getting up to try to quiet them down, and the teacher looks like he wishes he could go get drunk.

After the first class—when I showed up in an outfit that cost at least four hundred dollars, and, boy, did I look out of place—I went home and dragged my old suitcase out of my closet. Now I dress in the jeans and tops I wore when I was waiting tables at Tony's Truck Stop in San Jose, back before I married Tom Lange. I worked there again after we got divorced, until the day his lawyer called and told me he was dead and I was rich. I've always felt bad that I didn't hear about Tom dying until after the funeral, so I didn't even send flowers.

We work on math the first half of each class. The teacher said the test even has algebra on it. Algebra! What do I need algebra for? I have so much money I don't even bother to balance my checkbook and all that takes is adding and subtracting, which I'm good enough at as long as I can write it down. I'm also real good at computing fifteen percent because I used to check my tips to see if I was being stiffed. Which I was a lot of times. Truckers are nice guys, but some of them are pretty damn cheap. Travelers are worse. They know they aren't ever coming back again.

The teacher started droning on and on about common denominators and I started daydreaming about last night with Jonathan, only after a while Jonathan sort of morphed into his father. Charlie may be a ghost but he's a sexy ghost, and I was just about to find out what he wore under his bellbottom jeans when the sound of shuffling papers and sliding chairs brought me back to the real world. Break time. Lousy timing. Charlie faded away just like a ghost in a movie.

When Charlie's really here—not just in my daydreams—he doesn't fade away, he just disappears like magic. One second he's there, the next second there's nothing but air. He can't touch anything in the real world, so he was pretty useless last time he was here. I mean, a ghost would be pretty handy if he could bop the bad guys on the head, but what good's a ghost if all he can do is talk to you? Now, if he could do the things I'd been daydreaming about . . . Wow! But I wouldn't remember it for long, because when Charlie went away last spring he fixed it somehow so I forgot all about him. It wouldn't be long before I would start forgetting him again. In the meantime, I could use him in my daydreams.

I walked outside, following a group of my classmates across the street. The non-smoking mothers had hurried into the babysitting room but the smoking mothers needed a nicotine fix before they could deal with their kids, and half the guys in the class smoked. Smoking isn't allowed on the school grounds, not even after school is out, so they have to walk across the street before they light up.

I don't mind smoke, especially outside. The smell makes me lonesome for Duke, who smoked regular cigarettes after Lady made him stop smoking dope because she thought he was setting a bad example for me. Like I needed an example to be bad. I think maybe I would have done dope—I sure hung around with enough guys who did—if Duke hadn't spent most of my childhood getting high. Who wants to do something her father did?

The women smokers clustered together, sharing lighters and talking about boyfriends and husbands and kids and soap operas and their periods. The guys were in another cluster, not talking, just sucking in smoke and flicking ashes and sneaking peeks to see if the women noticed how cool they were. I walked past them and kept going, thinking maybe if I took a quick walk around the block I could pay attention to the teacher for the second part of the class instead of sitting there half asleep dreaming about sex with a ghost.

I had turned the corner when I thought again about how Charlie made me forget he existed. Right that minute I could remember everything about Charlie—everything that had happened in April and everything that had happened since I saw him standing by the bed last night. Every detail was clear. I wondered how long it would be this time before my memory of him started fading. By the time I'd told my story to a few cops in April, I believed it had really happened the way I told it, that Charlie hadn't had anything to do with it, that he had never been here. In a week or so I completely forgot he existed and I never thought of him again until he showed up last night.

I rounded the next corner, turning onto Oak Valley Street, the main drag through downtown. For some reason I glanced up and to my right and what I saw made me stop so fast my purse swung forward and then slapped back against my leg. My stomach flopped over and shivers ran across my scalp. Rachel Wright was smiling down at me from The Billboard.

CHAPTER SIX

Rachel Wright had braces on her teeth. If she'd lived long enough she would have had a very nice smile. But she was only ten and probably hadn't had the braces long at all and her teeth were still crooked, the front ones tilting toward each other, her eye teeth jutting forward. I never had to have braces. I was lucky and got Lady's teeth instead of Duke's.

Rachel had a turned-up nose, round cheeks, dimples, a curvy mouth, and big blue eyes. She would have always looked little-girlish, even when she was grown. Her short dark hair was permed, and too curly, like she'd had it done the day before just for the picture. Probably she had. Lady used to fuss something awful about my school pictures because she always gave framed eight-by-tens to my grandparents and put the wallet-sized ones in Christmas cards.

I don't think she ever showed anyone my last school picture, the one that was taken the month before I dropped out. I left the house looking like she wanted me to look, all scrubbed and shiny and much younger than sixteen. When I got to school I took out the dorky barrettes she'd made me wear to hold my long hair back, and I put on a ton of makeup and changed out of the white blouse with a lace collar that she'd bought me for

Picture Day. I thought I looked really cool with my hair hanging in my face and a skimpy tank top showing a lot of flesh.

When Lady saw the pictures she raised her hand like she was going to slap my face, but she didn't; she never did, although I think she must have felt like it a lot. She told me I looked like a tramp, and she was right but I couldn't see that then. I ripped the pictures up and threw them away when I cleaned out their trailer after they died. It made me cry, finding out that she'd kept them, and seeing how I really looked and knowing she was right. I don't think I'll ever regret anything as much as I regret not listening to my mother.

Rachel looked like someone's precious little girl, clean and combed and happy and innocent. She was wearing a pale blue blouse with lace trim on the collar. She was probably wearing a skirt, but the picture was just head-and-shoulders so I couldn't tell.

The picture on the billboard was huge and I stood there for a long time, craning my neck to look up at it. WHO MURDERED RACHEL WRIGHT? was written in big blood-red letters across the top. In smaller black print to the right of her picture it said:

> Rachel Wright, age ten, was kidnapped and murdered on Halloween Night in 1973. She was wearing a long white ghost costume. Three days later her body was found in a field on Rutgers Road two miles south of Oak Valley. Anyone with information about Rachel Wright or her killer should contact the Oak Valley Police Department Tip Line immediately at 555-9999. All information will remain confidential.

According to an article in the newspaper there was an identical billboard out on the highway but I hadn't seen it myself. The police also sent letters to churches, asking them to mention the murder during services, and they sent flyers to all the local businesses to put in their windows. There's even a picture of Rachel Wright on the bulletin board at the public library.

It wasn't clear in the article why the cops had suddenly decided to publicize the case again. Charlie hadn't really explained it either. Why now? Why hadn't they done this years ago? I wondered if maybe it was because of John Sterling, who had been a detective in April when Charlie Bilbo's murder was solved and who was promoted to Chief of Police because of that. He was a rookie cop in 1969 when Charlie died. He could have been involved in the investigation of Rachel Wright's murder four years later. Maybe since he'd solved one old case—with a lot of help from me—he figured he'd try to clear up another one.

I suddenly realized I was seriously thinking about going to the police department and asking Sterling about the case. I thought, *Damn you, Charlie, go away,* and turned around to go back to school. I'd wasted too much time looking at the billboard to finish walking around the block.

CHAPTER SEVEN

Just before the class ended, the teacher said, "You've all seen the billboard, I assume."

Some of the students murmured something or other. Everyone in Oak Valley had been talking about the billboard since it went up. You couldn't go anywhere without someone mentioning it, but I still felt creepy, like he'd read my mind. I'd been thinking about Rachel Wright ever since I got back to class.

"I was in one of the search parties," he said. "I spent a couple days trampling about in the woods north of town. I don't recall now why they thought she might be there. It was . . . I was young then. I'm not sure which I was more afraid of: that she would never be found, or that I would be the one to find her. The thought of finding her body terrified me." He sighed and added, "I hope they finally catch the person who did it. Class dismissed."

There was a lot of chair-scraping and paper-shuffling and throat-clearing but no one said anything and pretty soon I was alone in a classroom with a teacher. By choice, which was a first for me.

"Yes, Miss . . . Lange, is it?"

Actually it's *Ms.* Lange. I guess I was Mrs. Lange for a while since Lange was Tom's last name but I don't remember anyone ever calling me that, and I sure never felt like a *Mrs.* Before I married Tom I was Lizbet Dutton, Elizabeth Ann Dutton if you want the whole thing. Duke and Lady were hippies so it could have been worse. At least they didn't name me Starshine or Aquarius, or something really awful like Psychedelia Dutton.

"Lizbet," I said. "I was just wondering about Rachel Wright's murder. I suppose you know quite a bit about it."

He looked at me curiously. "May I ask what your interest in it is?"

"Um . . . I'm just curious." He began to gather up his books, shaking his head, like he thought I was hoping for some juicy gossip. I felt my cheeks heat up. "I'm curious because . . . because I have a lot of money and I was thinking about talking to the family and offering to put up a reward. You know, 'For information leading to the arrest . . .' That kind of thing." Now where did *that* idea come from? From Charlie, damn him. I hadn't even thought any more about his idea of offering a reward. I was just babbling out of embarrassment.

The teacher—I could never remember his name—stood there with an armful of books, staring at me for a moment, then he said, "You were in the paper last spring. Quite a help to the police, weren't you? The story mentioned that you're . . . wealthy. I've been wondering why you're here. Why not hire a private tutor, or just enroll in the community college? You don't need a diploma or a GED for that."

I was afraid of going to college, even junior college, afraid I'd flunk the classes and look like an idiot. But I didn't want to tell him that. "I thought I should improve my study skills first."

He smiled, and I noticed for the first time that he really wasn't a bad-looking man, sort of tall and lanky and boyish, like Jimmy Stewart in that old movie, *It's a Wonderful Life*, where

an angel shows him what would have happened if he'd never
been born. I think the mere fact that Mr. What's-His-Name
was a teacher was so intimidating that I never thought of him
as a person, let alone a man. "Well, Lizbet, maybe you need to
first work on paying attention in class. You seemed to be miles
away today."

He was a teacher after all. I thought about telling him that if
he'd make the class interesting I could pay attention, but I'd
have to drop out afterward and I didn't want to have to tell
Jonathan I'd dropped out of a dropout diploma class.

He moved toward the door, saying, "The library has the old
newspapers. You could take a look at them if you're interested.
As for the reward . . . it might help, who knows? Money can be
very motivating. Why don't you talk to someone at the police
department first. They would know how to go about it."

"Yeah, maybe I will." I followed him out the door, walked
to my car, then started home, passing by the billboard again. I
slowed way down so I could look at Rachel Wright's picture
again. It was getting to be an obsession or something.

CHAPTER EIGHT

As I headed home, I kept thinking about a reward. The billboard didn't mention one being offered now, and I didn't remember hearing anything about one being offered in 1973 either. The Wrights probably couldn't have afforded to put up the money themselves.

To get home from the high school I had to drive right through downtown on Oak Valley Street, which becomes Foothill Avenue when it starts winding up into the foothills of the Diablo Mountains, where all the houses are big and all the people are rich. Tom bought the house up there right after he got his money, which came from a lawsuit against computer companies. He died a few months later and I moved in.

Right in the center of town is the police station. I spotted an empty parking place in front of it, so I pulled in. I don't know why. After a minute I got out of the car and went into the building. I knew just where to find John Sterling. The office of the Chief of Police was on the second floor, right down the hall from the Detective Division, which is where Sterling's office was when I first met him. Now he's in a real office, not a cubicle. A secretary sat at a desk in the small outer office. She frowned at me, like she wasn't used to people just walking in and interrupting her. I told her I needed to talk to Sterling about the Rachel Wright case.

"And you are?" she asked.

The woman who made him Chief of Police. But I didn't say that, I said, "Lizbet Lange."

She wrote it down on a Post-it note, like it was way too hard for her to remember. Then she picked up her phone and tapped a button. "Chief Sterling? There's a woman here to see you about the Rachel Wright case. Her name is—" she used one finger to turn the Post-it note slightly—"Lizbeth Lange."

"Lizbet," I said. She ignored me. I wished I'd gone home first and changed clothes instead of coming here in old faded blue jeans and a baggy red T-shirt with Mickey Mouse on the front.

Sterling must not have had much to say because she put the phone down right away and said, "Go on in."

I walked past her desk and opened the door to Sterling's office. He was sitting at a big desk that was almost completely covered with piles of paper. To the side was a smaller desk with a computer monitor on it. The room smelled like very strong black coffee. A coffeemaker sat on the counter at the side of the room, an inch or so of dark coffee in the carafe. Sterling didn't smile or say hello, just watched as I closed the door and walked to his desk. I felt like a little kid standing in front of the teacher's desk, waiting to be yelled at.

"Hi," I said.

"Sit down," he said, gesturing toward a black vinyl armchair in front of the desk.

I sat. Sterling clasped his hands on the desk. "What brings you here?"

"Rachel Wright. I was wondering—"

"That's what Rosemary said. You make me nervous, Ms.

Lange. We get the first ever break in the Wright case, and within a few hours you walk in. Tell me this is a bad dream."

"You found out who killed her?"

"No. Did you?"

"Of course not. I was just wondering—"

"Because you can't know anything about it, right? You were what? an infant in 'seventy-three? No, you weren't even *born* yet, were you?"

"No, but—"

"Then why are you here?"

"Jeez, if you'd let me finish a sentence. I don't know anything about it, I just—"

"You didn't know anything about Charlie Bilbo either but that didn't stop you, did it?"

"*Chief* Sterling, you'd still be *Captain* Sterling if I hadn't figured out who killed Charlie."

"I would have figured it out eventually."

"Yeah, after his killer killed *me*. I was wondering—"

"So why are you here, Ms. Lange?"

I almost got up and left right then. I didn't understand why he was being so snotty. I helped him solve Charlie's murder, and he got promoted because of it, and now he was acting like I was nothing but a nuisance. But I didn't get up. I didn't say anything else, either.

After a while, he sighed and said, "Why are you here?"

"Are you going to listen?"

"I'm all ears."

"I was wondering if I could offer a reward. You know, for information."

"A reward."

"You know, I'd give some money to anyone who—"

"I know what a reward is."

"Well, don't you think it's a good idea?"

"I think you're scaring the hell out of me."

I realized I was clenching my hands together so tight they hurt. *Cops* scare the hell out of *me*. I wished I'd never come. "I haven't done anything," I said.

"No, but why do I have the feeling I'm going to be tripping over you every time I turn around? This case does not involve you. You have nothing to do with it. You have nothing to do with any police case, except maybe the case of the unpaid parking tickets. Why don't you pay them?"

Shit. "I will, I just keep forgetting. I only have a few."

"Six. You have six unpaid parking tickets."

"Is that what you do all day? Check up on my parking tickets? Seems to me the chief of police should have something more important to do with his time."

"Small town, Lizbet. I like to keep an eye on chronic offenders."

"I am not a chronic offender. They're *parking* tickets, for pete's sake."

"And if they're unpaid for a certain period of time they become warrants. If you're stopped for a traffic violation, you'll come up in the computer as having outstanding misdemeanor warrants."

"For *parking* tickets?"

"Yes, for parking tickets."

"I'll pay them today."

"That would be wise. It's not as if you don't have the money. I don't know why you let them go so long."

"They just don't seem important, and I forget about them. Do you mean I could go to *jail*?"

He shrugged, then said, "Speaking of money, why are you dressed like that? It's a bit, um, understated for you, isn't it?"

"Is there a law against how I'm dressed? If not, it's none of your business." I wasn't about to tell him I was dressing down so I wouldn't feel so out of place in my dropout diploma class.

"Point taken. Feel free to dress however you want." He made a sweeping gesture with his hand, a magnanimous gesture. Magnanimous! That was one of the words in the vocabulary list for the class! Maybe I was learning something after all.

Sterling suddenly smiled at me. He looks sort of like Sean Connery, not in the James Bond movies but in the Indiana Jones movie when Connery was getting old and played Harrison Ford's father. I wasn't sure how old Sterling was, in his late forties at least. "You look like a million dollars, Ms. Lange, even in blue jeans."

I was startled and felt myself blush. I muttered, "Thank you."

"Now about that reward idea of yours. Why don't I check with the family, see if they have any thoughts on the subject. I don't think it could be offered through the police department. It would have to be some sort of private arrangement. How much did you have in mind?"

"Um, I don't know. Ten thousand? Twenty thousand?"

"Nice round figures, both of them." He sighed, probably thinking how unfair it was that I had tons of money and hadn't done anything to earn it, just married a man old enough to be my grandfather.

"What was the break?" I asked.

He looked at me suspiciously. "The details of an ongoing investigation are confidential. Now, if that's it, I do have some work to do."

"Checking the list of chronic parking ticket offenders?"

He smiled again, then stood up and walked around his desk. I stood up and he took my arm and guided me to the door, like maybe I couldn't find it on my own. As I walked out, he said, "Drop by any time."

Not any time soon, I thought. I was going to ask his secretary how to pay parking tickets, but she was on the phone so I didn't.

CHAPTER NINE

I made another stop before I headed home, at Scaredy Pants, a temporary costume shop that opens up every fall in the back room of Jill's Jeans 'n Things. The same room turns into Wedding Belles, Holiday Frocks, Prom Pretties, and Mermaid Madness at other times of the year. Jill told me once that if everyone died at the same time of the year she could do a good business with Graveside Gladrags. I suggested Custody Costumes for the divorce season.

My costume was ready. I put it on in the tiny dressing room, then stepped out to look at myself in the big three-sided mirror. "Perfect," Jill said. She looks like an elf, short and round, with bright blue hair cut in a ragged zigzag around her face—her hair's a different color every time I see her—and a pug nose and a mouth that looks like she's smiling even when she isn't. She always wears outfits that match her hair, and lots of jangly jewelry.

She was right about my costume, it *was* perfect. I was wearing black tights and a black long-sleeved leotard that had a red hourglass shape on the front and four extra legs attached to the sides—my own arms and legs were the other four legs. When I told Jonathan I was going as a black widow spider, he grinned and said, "They eat their mates, right?" I said only in his dreams if he made any cracks like that at the party.

The leotard also had a tight-fitting black hood, which was kind of a shame because my hair is so pretty, reddish-gold and chin-length, cut in layers so it has lots of bounce—Monsieur Jacques himself does it for me and it always looks good; all I have to do is fluff it up with a brush after it dries. The hood came down on my forehead in a widow's peak, and curved into two points on my cheeks, like widow's peaks turned sideways. The hood was attached to the leotard, which had a high neckline like a mock turtleneck, so except for the very front of my face I was all covered in black, and at the party I'd be wearing a cloth Lone Ranger-type mask. I moved my arms up and down, watching my spider legs in the mirror. A length of clear plastic thread—like fishing line—connected each lower leg to the one above it, and another thread connected each upper leg to the sleeve of the leotard at my wrist. They worked like puppet strings; when I moved my arms, the spider legs followed.

"Look what I found," Jill said, appearing beside me holding a pair of black ankle boots.

The leather was very soft and supple. *Supple* was another one of my vocabulary words. Pretty soon I'd be using so many big words no one would know what I was talking about, including me. "Oh, I like them. I was going to wear black heels, but who ever heard of a spider in high heels? Are they my size?"

"Of course. Try them on just to be sure."

They fit fine. I said I'd take them, but thought I might go with the high heels anyway because they made my legs look a mile long. Still, the boots would be more comfortable for dancing. Maybe I'd just wear the heels for Jonathan for our after-the-party party. He'd never figure out how to get me out of a leotard and tights. He has enough trouble with bra hooks.

Jill suddenly said, "Have you seen that billboard they put

up? It just gives me the creeps. Do you think they waited until October on purpose? I mean, it happened at Halloween. Did you know I'm related to her?"

"To Rachel Wright? No, how?"

"She was my mother's cousin. Pretty big age difference; my mother was already grown when Rachel . . . died. So she'd be my second cousin. I think. Those things always confuse me. You know, second cousin, third cousin, cousin twice removed, all that."

"I don't understand it very well either. I don't have any cousins though because both my parents were only children. Well, Duke had a brother but he died when he was a kid."

"Duke?"

"My father. So you must know Rachel Wright's folks, right?"

"Oh, yeah. Rachel's mother is my mother's mother's sister's daughter. Oh, wow. Try again: Rachel's mother is my grandmother's sister's daughter."

So Rachel was Jill's grandmother's niece. Jill's mother's cousin. Jill's second cousin. Sometimes not having many relatives makes life easier. I just have my grandparents, and some great-aunts and -uncles on Lady's side of the family but I've only seen pictures of most of them because they live in Nebraska or someplace like that. Duke's and Lady's parents moved out to California about the same time but from different places in the midwest, and Duke and Lady were both born and raised in Gilroy. I guess I'm related to my great-aunts' and -uncles' kids, and their kids' kids, and maybe even their kids' kids' kids but I've never met them so who cares?

"Do you think you could introduce me to them?"

Jill's blue eyebrows shot up. "Well, gee, I don't know. I mean I don't see them very often myself, just at Christmas most years.

Sometimes Thanksgiving if someone's doing a real big family get-together, a reunion kind of thing, you know. There's nothing like that planned this year, at least not that anyone's told me about. Why on earth would you want to meet them?"

"I'm thinking about offering a reward. You know, for information leading to the arrest and conviction . . . That kind of thing. I already talked to the cops and they think it's a good idea."

"Oh, well, yeah, gee, that would be great. I mean, Rachel's parents don't have any money, not much money, I mean. Listen, I have your phone number. Why don't I talk to them and I'll get back to you?"

"Okay. Tell them I was thinking about maybe twenty thousand."

Jill looked stunned. She had to have known I had money, since I spent a whole lot of it at her shop, but she must not have realized I had Money with a capital M.

"I'll tell them, sure," she said.

After I changed clothes, Jill showed me the little hooks on the leotard sleeves where the plastic threads attached, then she unhooked them and ripped the legs off the leotard—they attached with Velcro—and then put the leotard and tights and mask and boots in a small bag and the four stuffed legs in a big white shopping bag. They stuck out the top.

"Be sure you put the legs on the correct side," Jill said. "Can't have a spider running around with her legs on backward. Not even a *rich* spider can get away with that."

I knew right then that shopping at Jill's Jeans 'n Things wasn't going to be much fun from now on because she'd be treating me different because now she knew I was stinking rich. Being rich has a few drawbacks. I'm not comfortable around rich people either, even if I am one myself. You always feel like you have to act classy and talk about something important and use the right fork. Rich people don't giggle. Jill and I had giggled together a lot and I was going to miss it.

I stuffed the smaller bag into the shopping bag with the legs and thanked her and went back to my car, and I was really planning to go home, but I drove by the library and instead of going on past I pulled into the parking lot beside it. I sat there for a while, then I locked up the Volvo and went inside, thinking I'd just take a quick look at the *Oak Valley Journal* from 1973.

I ended up sitting in front of the microfilm machine for over an hour, not even realizing how late it was getting until the lights blinked, signaling closing time. Eight o'clock. And I hadn't even had dinner. But I knew a lot about Rachel Wright's kidnapping and murder, including something that Charlie hadn't bothered to mention: Both Rachel's father and her uncle were Oak Valley cops in 1973.

CHAPTER TEN

I should have gone home. Instead, I sat in my car in the library parking lot as the other customers—patrons, they call us—left one by one, car doors slamming, headlights coming on. I was still there at eight-fifteen when the library employees left the darkened building and walked in a group to their cars at the far end of the lot. They drove past me, most of them slowing a little to take a look at the solitary car still in the lot, the woman behind the wheel. Maybe they were suspicious at first, thinking about burglary or vandalism, but then noticing that the car was a Volvo and driving on by. Whoever heard of anyone in a Volvo breaking into a library or spray-painting graffiti on public property? Good thing they didn't know about my juvie record. I stayed there, alone in the dark lot in my dark car, thinking about Rachel Wright.

The newspaper didn't call it a kidnapping, not at first anyway. They just said "disappearance" and later they said "apparent abduction." It wasn't until the big headline that appeared the day after they found her that they used the K-word: KIDNAPPED GIRL'S BODY FOUND.

On Halloween night Rachel Wright went trick-or-treating with her brother, four neighborhood children, and her mother, whose name was Brenda Wright. I think it was probably better that Rachel's own mother was the one with the kids, because it would be really awful for any woman to be responsible when another woman's child disappeared. Think how guilty she'd feel, and she'd always wonder if the parents blamed her. And maybe they would.

Laying the blame seems to be important when bad things happen. I guess we feel better if we can say "It's all *your* fault." I think that's why there are so many lawsuits. Everybody's looking for someone else to blame for their problems. When Duke and Lady died, I blamed them for not being careful, and I blamed the people who made the space heater, and the people who built the trailer, and I would have blamed the person who invented carbon monoxide, only nobody invented it, it's just there. I never thought about suing anyone though. I'd never even spoken to a real live lawyer back then. Poor Rachel's mother. I bet she blamed herself. I couldn't help but wonder if her husband had ever blamed her, if he had ever said, "It's all *your* fault."

And what about Rachel's brother and sister? Who had they blamed? I thought Rachel's brother had probably blamed himself because he was with her that night and he was her "big brother," ten months older according to the article. He was also in the sixth grade, in the same class as Rachel, because he hadn't skipped a grade like she had. Her sister was only two and had an ear infection, so she stayed home with their father. She wouldn't have even understood what was going on back then and she probably broke her parents' hearts by asking over and over where "Waychel" was. Later on though, when she was older, she would have tried to figure out who was to blame for her big sister being kidnapped right from under their mother's nose. How scary to realize that you aren't safe even with your own mother there to protect you. I bet those kids had nightmares for years.

Rachel Wright wasn't seen again—at least not by anyone who admitted it—until her body showed up in a field on the outskirts of Oak Valley. She had been dead for days, apparently murdered soon after she was kidnapped. The fact that her body was left in the open really puzzled everyone. Oak Valley was a small town then, and there were lots of country roads cutting through the forests around it. Why didn't her killer leave her in the woods, somewhere outside of town where she might not have been found for days, maybe weeks, maybe never? The guy who was chief of police then speculated that her killer wanted to get caught. If he did, he sure must have been disappointed.

The newspaper articles never actually said so, but I bet that the parents were the obvious suspects at first. I guess they always are, and that's pretty sad. But Brenda Wright had five other kids with her when Rachel disappeared, and her husband, Lawrence Wright, was home with their two-year-old and his wife's brother, Brad Hatcher, who was staying with them. The cops must have ruled out the parents and the uncle right away. They never came up with another suspect.

I leaned my head back against the headrest and closed my eyes and tried to imagine what it must have been like when Brenda Wright first realized her daughter was no longer with the group of kids she was leading from house to house on a chilly, drizzly, dark October evening. She would have felt panicky when she counted heads and discovered she was one short, and maybe her voice shook a bit as she called her daughter's name, wondering where on earth she was. Then she would have told herself she was being foolish: Rachel wasn't really gone, she had just strayed from the group, she had to be nearby. Maybe she was still at the last house. And Brenda Wright would have turned the group around, retracing their steps, calling her daughter's name, feeling a little angry at Rachel for giving her such a scare, trying to stay calm, trying to keep the children calm, telling her son not to be silly, his sister was somewhere nearby, Rachel was playing a joke on them, Rachel wasn't really missing.

But Rachel wasn't at the last house, she wasn't hiding in the bushes, ready to pounce out and shout *Boo!*, hoping to make her big brother look stupid for getting scared, and she wasn't running down the sidewalk toward her mother, crying, frightened because she'd gotten lost in the dark. She wasn't anywhere, and soon Rachel's mother was pounding on doors, running from one house to another, frantically calling her daughter's name, screaming her name, and people were coming out of their houses, pulling on coats, shouting questions, looking for Rachel, running into backyards and side yards, looking in parked cars, dome lights flickering on and off up and down the street, checking behind trees, yelling *"Rachel! Rachel!"* and some of them shouting that they'd called the police, and some of them trying to calm down Rachel's mother, who was hysterical by then, a terrified, sobbing woman surrounded by five crying kids.

Pandemonium. That's one of my vocabulary words. By the time the cops got there, it would have been pure pandemonium, a whole neighborhood of people searching for Rachel, calling for Rachel, all the porch lights on and flashlight beams sweeping behind bushes and trees and across dark yards, and people in their cars driving slowly down the streets, angling their headlights at trick-or-treaters who were suddenly scared of something more real than skeletons and vampires. A child was missing, the news passing quickly from house to house, from tin man to witch to fairy princess to pirate, from parent to parent. And all the children thinking it could have been them, and all the parents thinking it could have been theirs.

And Rachel's mother was no longer calling out her daughter's name, no longer even trying to tell herself that everything would be all right, no longer believing that Rachel was safe, just sitting slumped beside a jack-o'-lantern on the cold porch steps of a stranger's house, five scared kids huddled around her, her son's hand gripped too tightly in hers, her voice hoarse from shouting, but not shouting anymore, just whispering Oh, god, oh, god, oh god oh god oh god oh god, a mother with a missing child.

CHAPTER ELEVEN

I was going home, honest I was. I pulled out of the library parking lot and headed west and made it as far as Division Street, where Oak Valley Road's name changes to Foothill Avenue. Heading home, that's what I was doing. But I remembered the address, the Wrights' address. It was easy to remember because it was so simple, and also because when I saw it in the newspaper I thought maybe towns shouldn't have a 13th Street, the way some buildings don't have a thirteenth floor. I knew exactly where the house was, too. All I had to do was make a U-turn and go back seven blocks to 13th and hang a right, and twelve blocks down I'd find 1212 N. 13th Street. So I hung a U-ey. Don't ask me why.

As I parked in front of the house, I told myself that Jill had probably called Rachel's parents already, so it wouldn't be too rude of me to show up and talk to them about the reward. I was already out of the car when I realized that although a light was on over the front door the rest of the house was dark. Oh, well, it probably wasn't a good idea to stop by anyway. I was going to get back in the car, honest, except that I noticed that the front door was open a little. Then a gust of wind blew hard against me, and the door banged against the jamb and popped open again. It probably hadn't caught when they left the house.

Then a light came on in the Wrights' house, not in the front room but somewhere beyond that, the light just a pale glow through the thin drapes on the big front window. It was a small two-story house, two or three bedrooms and a bathroom upstairs; living room, kitchen, and dining room downstairs. Maybe a half-bath and a laundry room off the kitchen.

I looked around at the other houses. Most of them had lots of lights on and there were cars in the driveways and some parked at the curb. One car was in the driveway of 1212, a pickup truck actually, an old one with a dented tailgate.

I got out of the car, wishing I'd brought a jacket because it had cooled off a lot now that the sun had gone down and the wind had come up. I walked up the driveway, turning before I reached the garage to follow the short sidewalk to the front door, which was sucked outward by the wind again just before I reached it. It banged against the jamb and popped back open a couple inches. I saw what the problem was: the deadbolt was in the closed position, jutting out from the edge of the door, hitting the doorjamb each time the wind pulled the door closed.

Standing there on the doorstep in the weak yellowish glow from the light fixture above the door, I suddenly felt . . . *exposed*. And scared. I actually thought about digging my cell phone out of my purse and calling 911. But why? What would I tell them? I remembered about Mr. Wright being a cop, and I felt safer. He was probably retired by now, but a cop is a cop forever.

I turned and looked up and down the street. Down the block, at the house on the corner on the other side of the street, a man walked across the lawn. He stopped for a second, looking at me, I thought, but he must have decided I wasn't too suspicious because he got in the passenger side of a car parked on the street and the engine started right away and the car drove off, the driver remembering the headlights right after he turned the corner. I heard another car engine and watched as a car approached from the opposite direction. The driver pulled into a space behind a minivan that was parked two houses down. The headlights went out, but nobody got out. Kids, I thought, kids who'd been out on a date, staying in the car to make out for a while.

I felt a little better knowing someone else was nearby. There was nothing to be afraid of. I was just being silly. It wasn't like it was the middle of the night. I checked my watch: 8:47. Not late at all. And someone was home; someone had turned on a light in the house. I pushed my thumb against the doorbell but didn't hear anything so I knocked on the door, my knuckles barely making any noise against the wood because the door swung away as I touched it. I was reaching for the doorknob so I could hold the door steady while I knocked again when I heard someone say something. I couldn't make out the words. Come in? Was that what I'd heard? I wasn't even sure if it had been a man's voice or a woman's.

I called out, "Hello? Mrs. Wright?" A big blast of wind pushed against my back and the door blew open and stayed. I peered into the tiny dark entry. I could see stairs ahead of me, and not really light but just a sort of less dark space at the end of a short hall, which I thought must lead to the kitchen. The living room would be to the right of the entry, where the big front window was. "Mrs. Wright? Mr. Wright?"

I heard the voice again. I couldn't catch the words but I thought he—or she, it sounded a little high-pitched for a man—was probably saying "Come in."

"Are you in the kitchen?" I asked, my voice sounding too loud in the darkness. "Should I come on in?"

I heard it again, just sort of a high-pitched mumble. She had to be telling me to come in. I stepped into the entry. There was a funny burny smell, like someone had just struck a big wooden match. I walked down the hallway and then I was in the kitchen. A light was on somewhere on the other side of an archway that led into another room, probably the dining room, but it didn't cast much light into the kitchen. I could make out the white refrigerator and stove and the long shape of a counter and the dark rectangle of a back door. I felt along the wall at my right and found a light switch. The light was dazzling, making me blink, and then . . .

Oh, god! Blood! Blood all over the brown tile floor and a man lying face down in it, his head not more than a foot from my feet. And a gun, a gun on the floor by his outstretched hand, like he was trying to reach it.

Footsteps! Oh, god, *footsteps,* quiet footsteps on the tile in the entry, footsteps coming down the hall. I stooped down and picked up the gun, my hands shaking, my knees weak, and I spun around and pointed the gun at the doorway and a man slid in, a man in a crouch, a man with a gun in his hand, a man shouting, *"Police! Drop the gun!"*

I didn't have to drop it, my hands were shaking so bad I couldn't hold on to it, it just slipped away, fell away, the cop's eyes following its path, the gun taking forever to hit the floor, like a slow motion movie scene, then a dull thud and a big *BANG!* and the cop shouting *"Fuck!"*, dropping his own gun, hopping around on one foot, his hands clutching at his leg, blood dripping down his fingers, *"Fuck, fuck, fuck, I'm shot!"* and two cops in uniform coming through the door fast, two guns pointing at me. I burst into tears.

Chapter Twelve

"You shot a cop. You *shot* a *cop.*" Chief Sterling was really mad. He was standing behind his desk, leaning forward, his hands pressed against the desktop.

I was in the same old chair in front of his desk. "I *didn't* shoot him, not really; it just went off. He told me to drop it, so I did. It isn't my fault it went off. I didn't shoot him. I wasn't even *holding* it when it went off."

"You *shot* a *cop.*" He stood up straight, then sat down, sighing and shaking his head.

I wiped the back of my hand across my runny nose, sniffling loudly. I knew my makeup was ruined, knew I had raccoon eyes from my mascara, and my lipstick was probably all over my chin.

"One of them frisked me," I said. "He put his hands all over me, on my . . . my breasts and he stuck his hand . . . . his hand between . . . between my legs. Aren't they . . . aren't they supposed to let a woman do that?"

"You just shot a cop, you're standing beside a dead man, and they're going to say, Oh, Miss, please just stand there quietly for thirty minutes until we can get a female cop down here to see if you've got another gun jammed down your panties. Get real, Ms. Lange."

"He *frisked* me. He—"

"I know what he did. He did what he was supposed to do. You don't like it, cry on your lawyer's shoulder. You *shot* one of them. What did you expect them to do? Offer you a hanky and pat you on the head? You're goddamn lucky both the uniforms didn't shoot you."

"I didn't shoot him, I didn't—" But I couldn't talk anymore, my breath was coming in trembling, sobbing gasps, and I couldn't get the words out.

Chief Sterling muttered something, then he said, "Stop crying, okay? It's over. Just calm down." He moved around some papers on his desk, then asked, "The door was open when you got there, is that right?"

I nodded, the back of my hand pressed against my mouth, trying to stop the sobs.

"So you went in. You walked up to a dark house, a stranger's house, just the porch light on, you saw the door was open, and walked right in. Did you leave your brains at home?"

"I just . . . I just . . . I thought I heard . . . and the light in the dining room came on while I was outside. One of the cops told me it was a light on a timer, but I thought someone turned it on, I thought someone was home. Someone alive, I mean."

"Why were you there?"

"I just . . . I was . . . going to talk to them, to Rachel Wright's . . . parents. About the reward, I was going to—"

"They don't live there. I told you I'd talk to them and let you know what they said."

"I know, but Jill said she'd call them and I thought—"

"Jill who?"

"Jill's Jeans 'n Things. I got my Halloween costume there. I buy lots of stuff from her. She said . . . She's Rachel Wright's second cousin and I told her about the reward and she said she'd talk to the parents and call me, but I knew the address because

I saw it in the paper and it wasn't all that late and I thought she probably talked to them already and I was just going to ask them about it, about the reward, if they wanted me to put up a reward. What do you mean, they don't live there? Their address was in the paper."

"What paper?"

"At the library. On microfilm."

"You were reading the stories about Rachel Wright's murder?"

"Uh-huh."

"That was over twenty-five years ago. They don't live there anymore."

I felt stupid. Why had I thought they'd still be there? Nobody lives in the same house that long. Well, except for my Grandma and Grandpa Dutton; they've been in the same house in Gilroy since the 1960s.

"Then . . . who was the man? The man on the floor?"

"Brad Hatcher. Brenda Wright's brother. The Wrights sold the house to him in the early 'eighties. They live in a condo over on the east side of town now. Hatcher doesn't live there anymore either; he rents the place. His last tenants just moved out. Looks like he was over there doing some painting before he rented it again."

"Why would someone shoot Rachel's uncle? He's a cop, right?"

"He was. He retired a few years ago. You said you heard something. What?"

"A voice. I thought—I couldn't make out the words. I thought someone was telling me to come in."

"He was dying, probably died right about the time you were shooting Detective Flynn. Maybe he was moaning, or just breathing noisily. I don't think he could have been conscious enough to talk."

"You don't think . . ."

"What?"

"Well, that the gun going off . . ."

"Scared him to death?" Sterling smiled a little. "He was dying, Ms. Lange, would have died whether you'd been there or not. Even if the paramedics had arrived while he was still breathing, he'd have never made it to the hospital alive. Maybe it wasn't a voice you heard, maybe it was the dog."

"There was a dog? I didn't see one."

"He was in the dining room, hiding behind some paint cans. Gunshot must have scared him. Little dog, cockapoo, I think they're called. Not much of a watchdog. One of the neighbors said Hatcher'd just got it recently, had it with him the last few times he came to the house."

"Maybe it was the dog. It was just . . . like a voice, but not clear. Maybe it was the dog growling, or whimpering. How . . . why did the cops come?" I suddenly remembered the car that had parked down the street. Kids, I'd thought, but that must have been Detective Flynn's unmarked car.

"One of the neighbors called in a report of a gunshot. The uniforms were dispatched to check it out. Most gunshots turn out to be cars backfiring, but Flynn was in the neighborhood so he swung by anyway. He saw you by the door and watched to see what you were up to, and when you went inside he thought maybe you were up to no good. The uniforms arrived on the scene right after you went in. Flynn should have waited, should have at least sent one of the uniforms around back, but I guess he figured he had backup so he entered the building. He said he smelled gunpowder as soon he got in the door, that's why he pulled his weapon."

"Oh, yeah. I thought someone had lit a match."

Sterling sighed. "Ms. Lange . . . You probably missed the

killer by four or five minutes at the most. Do you understand that? Do you realize that if you'd shown up a few minutes earlier you might have gotten in his way, you might have been killed, too?"

Of course I knew that. Why did he think I couldn't stop shaking? I nodded, since he seemed to expect me to answer.

He sighed again. I wondered if he always sighed a lot or only when I was around.

There was a commotion on the other side of the door, and then Jonathan was there, pulling me up from the chair and hugging me so tight I could barely breathe, but I thought if he kept holding me like that I would finally stop shaking. With his cheek pressed to the side of my head, he said, "Why didn't you call me?"

I thought he was talking to me, but Sterling answered. "Calling the boyfriend isn't standard procedure, Officer Dillon. Ms. Lange didn't ask us to notify anyone she was here."

I felt Jonathan's jaw muscle tighten. I could also feel his badge and buttons and belt buckle and the edge of his holster or maybe it was his flashlight or nightstick. Being hugged by a cop in uniform isn't the most comfortable thing in the world. Plus, he was wearing his bulletproof vest—body armor, cops call it—so his chest didn't even feel like him. I pushed away from him. "I'm okay," I said. "I suppose every cop in the state is talking about me now."

Jonathan grinned, raking my hair away from my face with his fingers as he bent his head to kiss my forehead, then he let go and said, "Just about." Cops are worse gossips than women, and when a cop gets shot it takes about five minutes for every cop in the *country* to know about it.

"I didn't shoot him," I said. "I wasn't even holding the gun when it went off."

"I know." He grinned again. "I wish I'd seen the look on his face. Let's go home."

I looked at Sterling, but he spoke to Jonathan: "Stop downstairs on your way out and get her fingerprinted. We need elimination prints. She picked up a weapon at the scene of a homicide."

"The murder weapon?" Jonathan asked.

"We think so. It was fired twice. It belonged to the victim; he was a retired cop."

"Yeah, I heard. I'd sure hate to make it all the way to retirement and then get shot with my own gun."

"He might have always carried it—hard habit to break—or maybe he was expecting trouble. Looks like the killer got it away from him."

They started talking cop-talk, so I sat back down again, listening to them going on and on about calibers and latents and ballistics and all kinds of other totally boring stuff. I hitched my chair closer to Sterling's desk and crossed my arms on it and put my head down. I was almost asleep when Jonathan and Sterling finally noticed me and shut up.

"Ready to go, Lizbet?" Jonathan asked, as if *I* were the one who'd been yakking.

Jonathan's sergeant had told him to take the rest of his shift off. After all, a cop's girlfriend doesn't shoot a detective every day of the week. I didn't know where my car was—still on 13th Street, I supposed—so I rode home in Jonathan's car. We didn't talk on the way home, but I knew he was going to have plenty to say when we got there. But he held my hand tight all the way, except when he had to shift gears, of course.

CHAPTER THIRTEEN

Jonathan was very careful not to use the word *stupid*—"not very wise" is how he put it—but I knew he thought I'd been stupid to go into that house. It was hard to explain to him why I'd done it—it was one of those "you had to be there" things. I promised him I wouldn't do it again, not that it's the kind of opportunity that comes up every day.

I took a long bath while Jonathan sat on the edge of the tub. The San Jose cops knew an Oak Valley cop got shot within minutes of it happening since both police departments are dispatched by the county communications center, but the story Jonathan had heard was a little short on details. I explained how I ended up at the house the Wrights used to live in. He was very careful not to use the word *crazy*. "Unnecessary" is the word he used. "Let your lawyer handle the reward, Lizbet. It's a good idea, but you don't need to get involved in it except for putting up the money."

I got out of the tub and he dried me off and then I put on my warmest, coziest nightgown, floor-length with long sleeves, pale blue flannel with a pattern of tiny white flowers and white lace trim around the yoke and cuffs and collar. Jonathan always smiles when he sees me in it. He says I look like somebody in *Little House on the Prairie* when I wear it.

I was tired but Jonathan's used to being on duty until one in the morning and it was only eleven-thirty so he was wide awake. I got into bed and he tucked the covers around me and lay down beside me on top of the duvet.

"Jonathan?"

"Yeah?"

"One of them . . . one of the cops . . ." I started crying a little and couldn't talk anymore.

Jonathan raised up on an elbow, looking almost scared. "What's wrong? One of them what? What happened?"

I took a deep breath to calm myself down. "*Frisked* me," I said.

Jonathan stared at me for a moment, eyes wide open and blue, but not as blue as Charlie's. Then he very seriously said, "I'll find him and I'll kill him."

It was just what I needed, to kind of put it in perspective, you know? I shrieked with laughter. Jonathan laughed, too, and pulled me against him, tucking my head between his head and shoulder and holding me tight.

"I frisk women," he said. "I do it the same way I frisk a man and I don't get any thrill out of it. Actually, I don't do it the same way. I use the back of my hand, just pat her down with the back of my hand, so it's not so much like I'm groping her. Sometimes you can just grab handfuls of clothing and tell if there's anything hard under it. It's just a job, it's impersonal, I'm just checking for weapons, not feeling them up. I don't like doing it, I feel like I'm—I don't know what—intruding on them, I guess, but I do it because it's what I'm supposed to do, it's my job, and my life might depend on it, or another cop's life."

"I suppose a gay cop feels the same about frisking men, huh?"

"I guess."

"At least Sterling didn't arrest me," I said.

"What would he arrest you for?" Jonathan said, his chin moving against my head. "It was an accident."

"Well, I have some parking tickets . . ."

"Nobody gets arrested for parking tickets."

"He said they're warrants now."

"I'm sure they are, but we don't arrest people for them. The county jail's so overcrowded all we do is cite for warrants under five thousand dollars."

"Well, he made it sound like I could be arrested."

"He was yanking your chain, sweetheart. Why don't you just pay the tickets and stop worrying about them?"

"I keep forgetting."

Jonathan sighed. I seem to make men sigh a lot. After a while I went to sleep and he must have gotten up and gone downstairs because later on I woke up alone and when I called him, he didn't come. I thought about getting up and finding him, but I knew he was most likely using the computer in my library, surfing the Internet and checking out the cop newsgroups, so I stayed in bed and thought about his father.

I wasn't forgetting Charlie. Why wasn't I forgetting him? Good grief, what if I never forgot him? I didn't want to spend the rest of my life knowing ghosts exist. That could drive a person crazy, couldn't it? I mean, there are some things we just shouldn't know about and ghosts are one of them. If I didn't forget Charlie, it would have a truly profound—that's a vocabulary word—effect on me. I'd know that death isn't the end, that the dead can come back. I shivered just thinking about it.

I like to think there's a heaven and that Duke and Lady are floating around on a celestial cloud strumming harps, just as happy as can be, although Duke would be happier with a guitar. In heaven the crooked fingers he caught in the machinery at the cannery would be fixed and he could play the guitar again. I'd like to think they can keep an eye on me in some way, but not that they can actually see me and watch me pick popcorn hulls out of my teeth with my fingernail and things like that. I mean, what a horrible lack of privacy to have dead people hanging around watching you all the time.

Charlie fixes it so I don't go crazy when he shows up. I don't know how he does it, but he does. It's like the way he makes me forget him. Right now, my memory was as clear as a bell. That's a simile, a *trite* simile, old what's-his-name-the-GED-teacher would have told me, but a simile just the same.

I yawned a few times, then I whispered "Charlie?" Nothing happened. Why wasn't I forgetting him? Pretty soon I fell asleep, still worrying about it.

I had a horrible dream. I was in my Halloween costume with my four extra legs and I was caught in a giant spider web and Charlie was nearby, not in the web, but somewhere close, and he kept saying he had to frisk me and I kept telling him to shut up and help me. The sticky strands of spider goo were all over me, tickling my face and clinging to all my legs. In my dream, my extra legs were real. I could move them and everything, and it was confusing to have so many legs, and they kept getting stuck in the web. I'd work one loose but the others would be stuck tight.

Suddenly I wasn't in my costume anymore. I was wearing my long nightgown and only had my own two legs. A huge spider was stalking me across the web, or maybe it was a person wearing my costume. I tried to run, but it was like it always is in dreams: no matter how hard I ran I never got anywhere and the spider kept getting closer and closer and I was caught in the web and couldn't run, couldn't get away, couldn't even scream, although I tried to, and somewhere far away I heard Charlie's voice but I couldn't understand what he was saying.

I was still struggling in the web when Jonathan slid under the covers very slowly and carefully, trying not to wake me up. The dream vanished. I rolled over against him, wanting the warmth of his body. He slid an arm beneath me and pulled me close, saying, "I didn't mean to wake you up." I snuggled against him and after a moment he made a low growling sound in his throat and I giggled. He was naked and before long I was, too. A little while later he was panting right into my ear and the rhythm was picking up, faster and faster, and oh, it felt so good, so good, so good, and, oh, even better, and my whole body was tingling, and I was going to—

Tingling! My eyes popped open.

Charlie!

I said, "*God,* your timing sucks!"

And Jonathan said, *"What?"*

CHAPTER FOURTEEN

"I hope you realize you have absolutely ruined my life, Charlie. Jonathan's the only man I've ever known who treats me like I'm a person, like I'm *important*, not just somebody to . . . to . . . Well, Tom was really nice to me even when we got divorced, but Jonathan's the best man I've ever been with and you *ruined* it. He'll probably never speak to me again and it's your fault. All. Your. Fault."

"Why did you talk out loud? You know you don't need to."

"I was sur*prised*, you idiot. It's hard to remember not to talk out loud when you're just about to—when you're—when—when a *ghost* suddenly pops up by your *bed*. And that's the *second time!* You do it once more and I'm not going to believe it's an accident, I'm going to think you're some kind of pervert ghost and I'm never going to speak to you again, not *ever!* Out loud or *not*. And why are you back? And why didn't I start forgetting you?"

"You're my link."

"But I don't *want* to be your link. I told you I don't want to help you. I *can't*, Charlie. It just makes life so *complicated*. Normal people don't have ghosts. Look what happened—Jonathan's all upset because he thinks I was criticizing his . . . him, and I practically stepped on a dead man . . ."

Charlie was looking right at me, his eyes bright blue and

wide open and I couldn't look away. His eyes were so blue, so innocent. But he wasn't innocent; I knew that for a fact because I knew what he did before he died. Not innocent at all. I thought of the spider web in my dream, the sticky strands of silvery web clinging to me, holding me, trapping me, and I suddenly knew it wasn't a spider's web at all, and it wasn't just a dream. It was real, and it was Charlie's web. I was trapped in Charlie's web.

I forced myself to look away from him. It was ten o'clock in the morning and Charlie had just come back. Again. We were in the casual living room and I was still in my nightgown and robe, sitting on the couch with my legs curled beneath me. I started plucking at the nubby fabric of the couch cushion.

"I don't have a choice, do I? You just let me think I can tell you no. But I can't, can I? Even if I make you go away like I did in April, it's already too late, isn't it? Just like it was too late then. You left, but I was still all tangled up in your murder. It was too late because I was already involved, I already had the cops mad at me, and I already knew things I wasn't supposed to know, and the killer already knew I was a threat to him. And now it's too late again, isn't it? Because you changed things. Because you made me start thinking about Rachel Wright and I did things I wouldn't have done if you hadn't come here. I never would have even thought about a reward, I never would have gone to that house."

Charlie didn't say anything and after a moment I looked at him again, looked into his bright blue eyes, and said, "It's too late, isn't it?"

"Yes, I think it is. You're right, things have been changed. We have to finish it."

I sighed, really long and loud, just to be sure he knew I wasn't at all happy about this. "So what do I have to do now?"

"I don't know."

Big help. "Sterling said they had a break in the case. That was before Rachel's uncle was killed. I don't suppose you know what it was?"

"No. How would I know?"

"I don't know. You know things sometimes. When you want to. The rest of the time you're totally useless. If I have to have a ghost, why can't I have one that can help me?"

Charlie smiled, sort of a sad smile. *"I don't know. I just do what I'm supposed to."*

"That's what Hitler's guys said, isn't it? 'I was just doing my job'?"

After a moment, Charlie said, *"I don't really think that's a good comparison. I just know you have to be involved, you have to do something—I don't know what—to set things right."*

I sighed again. "And I'm just supposed to guess what it is? I'm really not any good at this, you know. I mean, I read mysteries sometimes and I *never* figure out who the killer is. So how am I supposed to figure out who killed Rachel Wright years and years and years ago?"

"Someone has to figure it out. Why not you?"

Which brought me right back to my original question: Why me? But there wasn't any point in asking him. I ignored him for a while, thinking about Jonathan. He'd been so confused and hurt, and he was half-mad and half-apologetic, and there was no way to explain what I'd said. I tried to pretend I'd been joking, telling him his timing was really so *good* that I just thought it would be funny to complain about it, just joking around, but it sounded really lame, you know, and I could tell he didn't believe me. He was gone when I woke up. Since he works late, he sleeps late, and when he stays with me he always sleeps until at least nine, but this morning I woke up at eight, just enough to realize he wasn't there, and then I got up and looked out a window and his car was gone. I couldn't go back to sleep. I don't think he even kissed me goodbye.

"You didn't tell me Rachel's father and uncle were both cops. Did you know them?"

"Yeah, I knew them."

"Is that why you're back?"

"I think that's just a coincidence."

"Pretty funny coincidence."

"Coincidences are always funny. We need to figure out what to do next." When I didn't answer, he said, *"The sooner we figure it out, the sooner your life will be back to normal."*

I wasn't sure my life had ever been normal. But it was sure less crazy when I didn't have a ghost in it.

"I guess . . ."

"What?" Charlie asked.

"I guess I'd better work on the reward some more, get it set up, you know? I should talk to the Wrights, but I don't know where they live."

"Check the phone book."

Now why didn't I think of that? They were in the phone book: 180 Pond Court. A condo, Sterling had said, on the east side of town. Wright's a pretty common name but the phone listing had both names—Lawrence and Brenda—so I knew it was the right one.

"Maybe I should call them first."

"No, let's just go over there. That way they can't refuse to talk to you."

"Why would they do that?"

"I don't know. I don't know that they would. It just seems better to see

them in person. Your friend at the store probably already talked to them, so they'll know who you are."

"See? You know about Jill. I didn't tell you about her so how do you know?"

He shrugged. *"I just do."*

I sighed again. Jonathan's always telling me that I need some structure in my life, that because I don't have to work I never get anything done because I have all the time in the world so I put things off. Like paying parking tickets. He told me I need to set some goals, like getting my GED and maybe going to college after that. I had a goal now: to get this whole thing over with in a big hurry so I could go back to my own life even if it doesn't have any structure and I never accomplish anything. What's wrong with just being rich? And I had goals, lots of them. Like finding a pair of shoes to go with this really cool dress I bought for New Year's Eve. It's deep blue, so dark that it looks black when there's no light on it, but then when light hits it, it turns shimmery midnight blue. The skirt is short and swirly and the top has a high neck in front and almost no back. It looks really great on me. It would be just my luck for Jonathan to end up working on New Year's Eve. I was a little nervous that he'd end up working on Halloween night even though he'd already arranged to have someone cover for him. San Jose cops work ten-hour shifts, so they only work four days and have three days off. Jonathan's always switching days off to help guys out who need to be at their kid's birthday party or something so a lot of times he doesn't have his three days off in row. But he promised me Halloween night, and he said he'll do the best he can about New Year's Eve. He doesn't really like parties though, so I don't know how serious he is about getting New Year's Eve off.

I sighed again, then I told Charlie to go away and I went

upstairs and got dressed, putting on a midcalf-length light blue dress that was sort of shapeless but looked good on me anyway. I tingled while I was putting on my shoes. Charlie was smiling when he appeared. I frowned. I really wasn't happy about this. I picked up my purse and said, "You're no fun, Charlie."

He laughed. There's just something about his laugh. I had to laugh, too.

CHAPTER FIFTEEN

Since the Volvo was still on 13th Street, we took the Porsche, which is bright red. I'm going to give it to Jonathan for his birthday because he's crazy about it and I don't really need two cars, three, actually, since my old pre-inheritance car is still in the garage, although I haven't driven it since the day the lawyer gave me the keys to Tom's cars.

We drove over to the east side of town and found Pond Court off River Road, which was the main drag through a whole neighborhood of condos where all the side streets were courts and they all had watery names: Lagoon, Lake, Loch, Waterfall, Cascade, Ocean, Channel, Brook, and on and on. It was enough to make you seasick. Pond Court was a short cul-de-sac and 180 was in the building at the end of it. There were eight units in each building, all two-story apartments, which is all condos really are except you buy them instead of renting them.

"Remember not to talk to me," Charlie said as we walked up to the door. On the drive over, I had decided I was never going to speak to him again. He kept complaining because I didn't have a map and we had to drive around checking all the street signs to find Pond Court.

I rang the doorbell and an old woman opened the door. It took a second for me to realize this was Rachel Wright's mother and the only reason I did realize it was that she hadn't changed

her hairstyle since 1973. It was still in a bouffant but it was thin
and gray, not dark like it was in the pictures in the paper. I know
it sounds silly but I had expected her to be young enough to be
Rachel's mother, and Rachel never got any older than ten. But
that was a long time ago. She must have been in her late twenties when Rachel died and now she was in her fifties. She was
tall and thin, her face all sharp angles, her eyes sunken, her mouth
a narrow line bracketed by deep creases. She was crying, her
eyes swollen and red. For just a second I thought she was still
crying over Rachel, but that couldn't be. Rachel died long ago.

"Better tell her who you are," Charlie said.

"I'm Lizbet Lange," I said. "Did Jill talk to you? About the
reward? I'm the one who wants to put up some money for a
reward. For Rachel. For . . ."

Brenda Wright started crying even harder.

"Who is it?" a man called from somewhere inside.

I heard him coming just as Brenda Wright said, "What are
you doing here?"

"I'm Lizbet Lange. Jill—Jill's Jeans 'n Things—she was going to call and—"

Lawrence Wright—Larry, I supposed—had appeared behind
his wife, putting a hand on her shoulder and sort of steering her
away from the door and back into the house. He was dressed in
a gray sweatsuit, and had thin graying hair. Rachel got her turned-
up nose and her big blue eyes from her father. With a wig and
some padding, he would have made a good Santa Claus, with
his short nose and round cheeks.

He looked a little startled. "You're the woman with the
money?"

"Yes. I'm Lizbet Lange. Is this a bad time? I could come
back—"

"Bad time?" He laughed but not like anything was funny. "It's been a bad time for a long time. Now it's worse. Come in."

Charlie and I followed him into a living room that looked more like a thrift shop than a home. Things were piled all over the place: stacks of magazines and books, folded clothes, straggly rows of cheap knickknacks on the end tables. Behind the glass doors of a china closet mugs and bottles and vases and little figurines were jammed in so tight you couldn't see the shelf they were sitting on. A bookcase stood beside the television, looking like it was about to collapse from the weight of all the books in it, some standing up, others flat on top of them, sloppy piles of paperbacks teetering on the top beside stacks of magazines. There were too many chairs, too many small tables, too many lamps, and the room smelled musty and dusty. There were no Halloween decorations; it wouldn't be a holiday they would want to celebrate.

Mr. Wright looked around the room like he'd never been there before, then he told me to have a seat. I chose a brown straight-backed upholstered chair that was placed at a right angle to an ugly brown-and-cream plaid couch with cushions permanently smashed from years of use. Mr. Wright sat down on the couch, sitting right on the edge of the cushion, not leaning back, and facing straight forward so he had to turn his head to look at me. Charlie stood beside my chair.

It suddenly occurred to me that I should have had my lawyer handle this. After all, that's what he gets that big retainer for. He handles all my legal stuff, like when Tom's other ex-wives and their grown children tried to contest the will and take the money away from me. He's a pretty good lawyer. He'd know how to handle a reward. Then I realized why I couldn't do that. Because the big idea here wasn't that I was going to be a do-gooder and offer a reward, the big idea was that I was going to solve Rachel Wright's murder. Because of Charlie. I shot him a dirty look. Mr. Wright saw me do it and looked puzzled. I guess it was a little strange for me to glance up and glare at nothing standing beside me.

"If this is a really bad time, I could come back later."

"There's no good time."

"So Jill called you?"

"Jill. Yeah, Jill called. She's some kind of relative of my wife's. Her cousin or something. We don't see much of her." He muttered something else I didn't quite catch, something about not seeing much of anyone, I thought.

"Yes, well, I thought maybe a reward would help solve your daughter's . . ."

"Murder. She was murdered. No sense in pussyfooting around it. It's been a long time." He looked toward a doorway leading into some other room, the dining room probably. All I could see was one wall and the side of a big chest or bookcase and a stack of cardboard boxes next to it, the top one open, a bunch of stuff piled in it higher than the sides. Mrs. Wright was somewhere in that direction, sniffling and sobbing.

"Well—"

Mrs. Wright's sobbing rose to a higher pitch.

"I need to—" But Mr. Wright didn't seem to know what he needed to do. He sat with his hands clenched between his knees. "Her brother died last night. Killed. Someone shot him."

"Oh, jeez, Charlie, that's why she's crying. I didn't even think about it! Her brother just got killed and we show up to talk about money. No wonder she's crying." I was kind of relieved though. I'd been thinking she was still crying over Rachel after all these years. *"Why didn't you remind me?"*

"I didn't know you'd forgotten."

I glared at him again, and Mr. Wright's eyebrows were raised when I turned back toward him.

Charlie said, *"Try to pretend I'm not here."*

I thought about telling him to just go away, because it was really hard to remember not to react to him when he was standing there beside me. But I didn't want to be alone with this man and his crying wife.

"I'm sorry," I said, "I'm sorry about your wife's brother." Should I mention I'd been there? The cops must not have told him. He'd find out eventually and wouldn't he think it was funny if I didn't mention it? "Um, I was at the house last night, the house on Thirteenth Street." When he didn't say anything I added, "I found him on the floor."

Mrs. Wright had been coming closer, her sobs getting louder. She appeared in the doorway, a big wad of tissue in one hand, her voice a little shrieky as she said, "You were there! Why were you there?"

Mr. Wright stood up, his shins bumping into the coffee table, sending a stack of magazines slithering sideways, a few of them sliding onto the floor.

His wife said, "You're that woman! You were at the house! What were you doing there? You didn't know him, did you? Why were you there?"

Mr. Wright rounded the coffee table, heading toward his wife.

"I didn't know him. I went there because I thought you still lived there and I wanted to ask you about the reward."

Mr. Wright put his arm around his wife's shoulders and patted her awkwardly. "The police department contacted us last night. They told us a woman found him. Lange, yeah, that's right, a woman named Lange. You were looking for us? We haven't lived there in years. We sold it to Brad."

"Yes, well, I know that now. The police told me. It was just sort of an accident that I was there."

"This reward," Mr. Wright said, his fingers kneading his wife's shoulder, "how much are you talking about?"

"I thought maybe twenty thousand."

"Twenty thousand dollars." He said the words slowly, sounding like he couldn't believe anyone really had that much money to spare. "There wasn't any big reward back then. Five thousand, that's all we could come up with, all we could have borrowed on the house if we'd had to pay a reward."

His wife wailed.

I thought about the stories in the newspaper, about all the people who searched the woods day and night, looking for Rachel. Maybe if Rachel's body hadn't been found so soon someone would have put up a reward. But once people knew she was dead, it was over. There weren't even very many stories in the newspaper after that. Some other story came along, some other tragedy, and Rachel wasn't real to them anymore, she was just a story they used to scare their children on Halloween night. No more real than the bogeyman.

Brenda Wright stopped wailing and blew her nose. "Would you like to see her room?" she suddenly asked me, still dabbing at her nose but sounding cheerful, like she'd forgotten she was crying.

"Whose room?" But I had a horrible feeling that I knew just whose room she meant.

"Why, Rachel's, of course. It's such a pretty room. Come with me. It's upstairs."

"Oh, I don't think—"

"Go with her," her husband said. "Go with her and look at the room. It'll just take a minute and then you can come back down." I looked at him and saw a pleading look in his eyes.

Humor her, he was telling me. I knew then that she *was* still crying for Rachel, that she'd never stopped crying for Rachel. I felt awful. Charlie and I followed her up the stairs, walking close to the railing to avoid the papers and clothes and books and skeins of yarn stacked against the wall on the bottom four or five steps. I thought they'd probably been there for years, waiting for someone to carry them upstairs. I felt like I was heading to a dentist's chair.

Rachel Wright's room was pink and white, with wicker furniture and puffy pillows and frilly curtains and quilts. On the bookcase headboard and on the pillows of the double bed were Holiday Barbies, still in the boxes, tall boxes with clear plastic fronts, some curved, some angled, ten or twelve Barbies trapped forever behind plastic; Barbies with impossible waists, and long, long legs, and feet permanently bent for high-heeled shoes; Barbies dressed in shimmery, shiny dresses, red and green and black and gold and white; Barbies with long blond hair curled and twisted and twirled and looped.

Boxes of Barbies stood on the dresser and chest of drawers, two more Barbie boxes sat on the seat of a white wicker rocking chair, a row of Barbies in boxes stood on the floor, lined up against the wall. Older Barbies, not in boxes but looking new, filled a big glass-fronted cabinet. Rachel only lived ten years but her room was decorated with at least thirty years' worth of Barbies. I felt a little sick.

Brenda Wright said, "I still get her a doll twice a year, for her birthday and Christmas. She loved them. They're collectibles, now, you know. Some of them are worth hundreds of dollars. You have to leave them in the boxes though. You can't take them out. They aren't *toys.*"

But they *were* toys. I remembered my own Barbies. I had five or six of them at least. I played with them, I dressed them and undressed them, and made them kiss my Ken doll, and I had weddings for them, and tea parties. I pushed them around the floor in a pink Barbie-sized Corvette and I combed their hair and when I got bored I took Lady's sewing scissors and snipped off their hair. I cut Malibu Barbie's hair so short Duke called her my butch-dyke Barbie. Duke wasn't very politically correct.

"They're . . . very nice."

"She's crazy," Charlie said. I couldn't really argue with that but I thought it was pretty tacky of him to say it. Good thing she couldn't hear him.

"Here's her album," Mrs. Wright said, thrusting a big pink photo album into my hands. Not long before she died, Lady and I went to a class to learn how to do photo albums like this one. The pages were three-hole-punched, made of acid-free paper, the photos held in by special double-sided sticky tape, and I knew the date would be written on the back of each photo or memento with a special pencil that wouldn't damage them. They sell all kinds of things now to make your albums special: fancy borders, and stickers for holidays and birthdays and other events, and even stick-on comic strip balloons to write on. Lady and I each did one page at the class, and then we never did another one. I felt sad now, seeing Rachel Wright's beautiful album, knowing that Duke and Lady's old photo albums were stuck on a closet shelf, the photos held in with those little black triangular corners, the scrapbook pages full of acid, probably eating away at the pictures right this minute. Most of my own pictures are stuffed in a shoe box on that same closet shelf.

In Rachel's album the corners of photos were clipped into curves or zigzags and some of the pictures had been cut into ovals or circles, all the ugly things you never realize are in the background until they are trimmed away. Each page was decorated with pretty stickers—flowers, balloons, butterflies, hearts.

Charlie stood beside me, looking at the pages as I turned them. On the first page there was a birth announcement and a birth certificate. The next several pages were Rachel's babyhood: baby Rachel in her crib, in a round pink plastic baby bathtub, in her father's arms; Rachel, propped against a slightly older baby— her brother, I assumed—with a grownup's hand at the edge of the picture, gripping her leg. Rachel in a stroller, Rachel all dressed up in a lacy pink dress, a bow on top of her head, Rachel with a pacifier, Rachel with a rattle, Rachel asleep on her tummy, her knees drawn up beneath her. Pages and pages of baby Rachel.

After that, the photos were grouped to show Rachel at different ages but in similar situations, the pages labeled SCHOOL DAYS, CHRISTMAS, HALLOWEEN, VACATION TIME, FAVORITE FRIENDS, and so on.

I turned pages: Rachel with chocolate all over her face, the remains of a birthday cake in front of her, a single candle tipped at an angle on it; Rachel on nine more birthdays. A tiny Rachel sitting on the floor in front of a Christmas tree, piles of ripped-off wrapping paper surrounding her; Rachel in front of Christmas tree after Christmas tree after Christmas tree, sometimes alone, sometimes with her brother, sometimes with other children—a tiny baby, two little boys, a little girl who looked a lot like Rachel—cousins, I thought, Brad's kids. Rachel as a tiny ballerina, then a princess, a blue bunny, a clown, a fuzzy pink rabbit, a vampire, a flapper, a cat, a witch. Rachel holding Easter baskets and Easter bunnies; Rachel at the table on Thanksgiving Days; Rachel on Fourth of Julys.

Rachel in a sandbox, in a little swimming pool, on a slide, on a tricycle, on a bike. Rachel in her mother's jewelry and makeup, in a swimsuit, in a fancy dress. Rachel with someone's infant on her lap, a big grin on her face, a front tooth missing, her brother sitting beside her, looking off to the side, looking bored. He looked a lot like Rachel, but her features didn't work as well on him. The turned-up nose looked too small on him, too short, the bridge too flat, too much space between his nose and his upper lip. Rachel was cute, even with her crooked teeth, but her brother was just plain funny looking.

I turned some more pages: Rachel on the wharf in Monterey, on the beach in Santa Cruz, waving from a cable car in San Francisco, in front of a huge sequoia; Rachel shaking Mickey Mouse's hand, black mouse ears on her head. Rachel peering out the window of a big yellow school bus; Rachel on a stage with other children, their faces framed by construction paper flower petals. Rachel in family portraits, in snapshots with her eyes closed or turned strangely red by the flash, Rachel in school pictures. Rachel growing up, but not too far up: the last page had an eight-by-ten copy of the school picture that was on the bill-board: Rachel at ten, not long before she died.

I closed the book and held it out to Mrs. Wright. "It's very nice."

Mrs. Wright held the book with one hand, stroking the front cover with the other, the way you'd stroke a cat. "She was . . . such a good girl." Her eyes filled with tears again.

Mr. Wright was at the door of the room. I hadn't heard him come up the stairs but I sure was glad to see him. I felt like I was being rescued. "Come on," he said. I said thank you to his wife and followed him back downstairs, leaving Mrs. Wright crying in her dead daughter's room. Somehow it wouldn't have seemed so crazy if it had actually been Rachel's room once, and her mother had kept it like a shrine. But Rachel had never even lived there.

Chapter Sixteen

"You shot one of the cops, huh? Musta scared the hell out of him." Mr. Wright grinned and for just a second I saw the man he used to be, the man who didn't have a daughter who was dead and buried at ten, who was gone forever before she was grown.

"Do you know him? Detective Flynn?"

"No, I've been retired for nine years now, closer to ten, I guess. Haven't really kept in touch with anyone." He cocked his head, listening to his wife's sobs. "When you lose a child," he said, "when you lose a child . . . it never ends. Nothing ever ends."

"I'm sorry, Mr. Wright. I'm really sorry about Rachel."

He smiled again, a sad smile this time. "Call me Larry."

"So, it's okay with you if I offer a reward?"

"Oh, sure, sure. We appreciate it."

"Find out where the brother lives," Charlie said.

"Why?"

"We might need him."

I didn't need him, and I sure didn't want to meet him. Good grief, wasn't it bad enough that I had to meet her sad father and her crazy mother? "Where does your son live now?" I asked Mr. Wright.

"Here. He lives with us. He . . . helps sometimes. With his mother. She . . . she has bad days. I need to get away now and then. He looks after her when I'm gone. Fishing. I go fishing."

I thought that was weird: a grown son living with his parents. I mean, you're supposed to grow up and move away and get on with your own life, right? But maybe it's different if your mother's nuts. Still, it didn't seem right to me, not healthy, you know?

"He works swing shift, gets off at three in the morning, he's probably still asleep. Did you want to meet him for some reason?"

No, I didn't want to meet him, I definitely didn't want to meet him. I didn't have a chance to say anything because Mr. Wright suddenly said, "Speak of the devil," as a door opened and closed on the second floor and I heard footsteps overhead. A man came clumping down the stairs.

I had that time-out-of-kilter feeling again, like I'd expected him to be a kid but he had gone through a time warp, reaching his middle thirties while his sister was still ten. Like Rachel, he took after his father, but he wouldn't have made a good Santa Claus. He was too thin, his face narrow and bony, his short nose looking all wrong without the round cheeks to go with it. He must have seen me on his way down—we were standing in the entry at the foot of the stairs—but when he reached the last step he did a double-take, like he'd just noticed me standing there.

"Ryan, this is Lizabeth Lange. She's the one's going to put up a reward."

Ryan Wright. They really liked those R-sounds, didn't they? Rachel Wright and Ryan Wright. I wondered what the little sister's name was. Rebecca? Ruth? Rhonda? At least they hadn't spelled the kids' names Wrachel and Wryan.

"It's Lizbet," I said. "How do you do?" Ryan Wright shook my hand, grinning quickly, but he was looking at his father, not at me. "Well," he said, glancing at me, his eyes darting quickly away. Then he said, "What is it?" to his father.

"Nothing. She just wanted to meet you."

"Well. Okay."

"Your mother's having a bad day."

Ryan didn't answer. He was probably used to his mother's bad days; after all, she'd been having them for decades now.

"She's talking about twenty thousand dollars."

"Yeah?" He looked at me with a lot more interest, kind of giving me the once over, trying not to be too obvious about it. "Well, maybe that'll . . . maybe someone will want the money. I don't know though, Dad. I mean, it's been so many years. It's too late for something to turn up now, some evidence. I don't know why they even bothered with that sign." Ryan was twitchy, in constant motion, rubbing a hand up and down his pants leg, then rubbing his chin or his forehead or pulling at the neck of his blue t-shirt. He had an odd way of grinning quickly while he was talking, even though nothing was funny.

"Well," I said, "they put the billboard up and the next thing you know, Rachel's uncle is murdered, so maybe—"

"What does Brad have to do with it? He doesn't have anything to do with it." Larry Wright looked shocked, like he'd never even considered there was a connection.

Ryan said, "I think Paula shot him. They fight a lot."

"I talked to her—That's Brad wife, Paula," Larry said to me. "Widow now, I guess. Anyway, she was at her Weight Watchers meeting when he was killed, came home to find a cop on her doorstep." He looked at Ryan. "You should have gone with us to see her, called her at least."

"I didn't see her when Brad was alive." Ryan grinned once, twice, a third time. It was almost like a tic, like he didn't even know he was doing it. "She doesn't like me, Dad."

"Well," I said, "I really need to be going. I'll find out how to set up the reward. I hope it helps."

Larry said, "Brad being killed . . . I don't think it has anything to do with Rachel. Brad was . . . he was the kind of guy who liked to rub people the wrong way, just to get to them, just to make them mad, you know what I mean? He made a lot of enemies."

I nodded.

"Rachel's murder . . . The worst thing is . . . the worst thing is never knowing. Never knowing for sure."

For sure. Did that mean he suspected someone? Maybe this was a clue. I looked at Charlie, who smiled at me; maybe he was thinking the same thing.

I suddenly remembered something I'd read somewhere, something about most murdered children being killed by someone they know, a member of their family or a friend of the family. They teach you about "stranger danger" in school; maybe they should teach you about "friendly danger" instead. I shivered, and I wanted more than anything to get out of there, to get away from these people.

"I really should be going," I said. "It was nice meeting you, Ryan. I'm sorry about . . . everything."

He offered his hand for me to shake again, not such a short shake this time, and he squeezed my hand just before he let go, and grinned three or four times, his mouth moving like a wind-up toy.

"Do you like movies?" he asked. "I go to the movies a lot."

"Uh, well, I actually mostly just watch videos. Gee, I'd better go. I'm going to be late if I don't go now. I'm meeting my, um, fiancé for lunch. He's a policeman."

"He is?" Larry looked interested. "Here in Oak Valley?"

"No, in San Jose."

Ryan seemed to have lost interest in us. He turned and started down the hall. His father said, "Funeral's tomorrow, Ryan, don't forget."

Still walking away, Ryan spoke in a whiny voice, sounding about ten. "I don't like funerals, Dad. People cry at funerals. I don't like—"

"You have to go, wouldn't be right if you didn't. Did you remember to call in and tell them you're taking tonight off? Funeral's at ten so you can't work tonight, you won't get enough sleep." Ryan had reached the end of the hall and turned a corner and was out of sight before his father finished talking.

Larry shrugged, then opened the door for me. We walked out to the curb, where he looked over his shoulder at the closed door of his house. I had the feeling he didn't want to go back in there. He thanked me again for the reward and I told him goodbye.

When we were in the car, Charlie said, *"You and Jonathan are engaged?"*

"No," I said, turning the key in the ignition. "Of course not. I just said that because Ryan was . . ." I didn't know how to describe how I felt about Ryan. His reaction to me just seemed all wrong. "I just wanted to discourage him. I thought he was going to ask me if I wanted to go to the movies with him."

As I put the car in gear, I glanced back at the condo. Larry Wright was still standing on the sidewalk, watching me. Watching me talk to myself in the car. Life with a ghost is just irritating, you know? I pulled away from the curb, heading back toward River Road.

CHAPTER SEVENTEEN

After I found my way back to Oak Valley Road, Charlie said, *"Have you thought about how odd it is that Rachel Wright disappeared when she was with her mother? I can't see someone snatching her from the middle of a group of kids and no one noticing, not with her mother right there."*

"Yeah, but . . . then what happened? Did she just walk away? Why would she do that? And how? Her mother would have noticed."

"Maybe her mother wasn't there."

I thought about that for a while. "But if she left the kids alone . . . why wouldn't she tell the police? I mean, she wanted them to find Rachel, right? Wouldn't she do anything she could to help them? If she wasn't there, if she left the kids alone even for a few minutes, then that changes the whole thing and if she didn't tell the police, well, she interfered with the investigation, she made it harder for them to find Rachel. Maybe she even got Rachel killed. Would she do that? God, how could she live with herself if she did?"

"She's not doing a very good job of living with herself, is she?"

"No. I know having your daughter killed must be really awful. I don't know what Lady would have done if anything happened to me. But you know what, Charlie? I don't think she would have gone crazy. I think she would have been horribly sad, and she would have missed me the rest of her life and she never would have forgotten me. But I think she would have gone on with her life. I don't think she would have bought dolls and fixed up a room for me and never stopped crying. That just isn't normal."

"And maybe guilt explains it better than grief."

Guilt. I thought again of Brenda Wright, walking down a dark street on a cold, drizzly October evening, suddenly realizing Rachel was no longer with the group of children she was taking trick-or-treating. She'd panic and frantically call for Rachel, but overriding her panic would be guilt, guilt because she'd left them, guilt because Rachel was gone and she hadn't been there to stop her, to stop whoever took her, guilt because even while she was praying for Rachel to turn up, she was telling Ryan and the other kids not to tell, don't you tell anyone I left you alone, don't you ever tell.

But why would she leave? How could she leave? The other kids would know. And even if she told them not to, wouldn't at least one of them mention it to the cops, or to their parents? I suddenly wondered how old the other children were. I didn't remember it saying in the paper. "What if the other kids were really little? What if they were so young they couldn't talk to the police?"

"Good question. We need to find out who they were."

"Their names weren't in the paper. I don't remember it mentioning their ages. Four neighborhood children. I think that's all it said."

"Maybe Sterling would tell you."

"I don't want to ask him."

"Why not? It couldn't hurt to ask."

"Maybe Jill knows. Let's go ask her."

So we drove downtown to Jill's Jeans 'n Things. Jill was waiting on two teenagers in the main part of the store, not the Scaredy Pants room. They were yanking clothes off the racks and holding them up in front of the big mirrors and oohing and aahing and giggling. Jill rolled her eyes at me a few times and finally sent the girls into a dressing room with a big stack of skirts and tops on hangers. She came over to the cash register, where Charlie and I were standing.

Jill was purple today, with tinkly silver bells draped around her neck and dangling from her ears. She had silver streaks in her purple hair and silver glitter on her purple eyelids. "You're back," she said. "Nothing wrong with the costume, I hope."

"No, it's fine. Listen, I talked to Rachel Wright's parents about the reward. I was just wondering . . . do you know who the other kids were, the ones who were trick-or-treating with them?"

"When Rachel was kidnapped? Good grief, why do you want to know?" She didn't wait for me to answer, which was a good thing since I didn't really know how I could explain it to her. "I could ask my mother; she'd know."

"Could you? I'd really appreciate it."

"Right now? Well, I guess . . ." She leaned over the counter and picked up a cordless phone, then tapped some numbers. She said, "It's me, Mom," then explained what she wanted and then said, "Uh-huh, uh-huh, uh-huh," while she scribbled some names on the back of a handbill about Scaredy Pants.

"Ask her how old they were," I said, and Jill nodded and asked.

After she hung up, she handed me the paper then stood beside me, pointing to the names as she told me about them.

"Tony Fenton, he works at the high school, teaches English, I think, and his sister Sandy. She's married, but Mom doesn't know her last name now. Billy Offenbach. Mom said they moved away years ago, the Offenbachs did. And Holly Brown, I know her. She works at the Oak Valley Bank. Her last name's Wood now. Can you believe that? Holly Wood. I always wondered if that's why she married the guy—so she'd be Holly Wood."

I was staring at the paper. "These are the ages? They were all three or four?"

"Yeah, little kids. Rachel and Ryan were a lot older. Ten, both of them. Brenda, their mom, she must've got pregnant practically the day she brought Ryan home from the hospital. Yuck. Can you imagine? Of course it was different back then. I don't think they even had the pill. Well, maybe, but I bet a lot of women weren't on it, and men, well, you know how they are."

"The late 'sixties."

"Huh?"

"That's when birth control pills were . . . invented or whatever."

"So maybe Brenda wasn't on the pill. I bet she was after Rachel was born though. Or maybe she just told the old fart to leave her alone. It was years before she had another baby. Seven or eight years."

"What's the little sister's name?"

"Uh . . . oh, god, what is it? . . . *Rebecca*, that's it."

Of course. Rachel, Ryan, and Rebecca.

The giggly girls came out of the dressing room and I thanked Jill, then Charlie and I went back to the car. We were parked in the tiny lot behind Jill's store and there was no one else around, just a bunch of parked cars, so I turned in the seat to face Charlie.

"They were little kids. I remember kindergarten, some of it

anyway. Before that . . . I remember a few things, like getting lost in a store and crying because I couldn't find Lady; I must have been three or four then. But I only remember being scared, not what the store looked like or who was there and I remember Lady getting mad at me for getting lost. Most of the stuff I know from when I was little I don't really remember. I just know about it from Duke and Lady talking. Like the camping trip we went on when I was three and I sat down in a big pile of bear poop. I don't remember it but Duke told me about it a hundred times. I don't think they'd remember anything, not anything they didn't tell their parents about back then."

"It would have been traumatic, having someone they knew disappear. They might remember it. We should talk to them."

Talking to them sounded like a stupid idea to me. What could they possibly tell us? I looked at Charlie, at the peace symbol on his chest and his long blond hair and his blue, blue eyes, and I realized his mouth was just like Jonathan's and I knew how it would feel to kiss him. I said, "The bank's right down the street. I guess we could start with Holly Wood."

But Holly Wood wasn't there; she'd called in sick. We went back to the car and I used my cell phone to call Jill and ask if she knew how I could get hold of the others. She said to call her back in five minutes. When I did, she told me she'd called her mother again. "She doesn't know for sure where the Offenbachs moved to, maybe Oregon. She couldn't find a phone number for Tony Fenton, must be unlisted, but he teaches at the high school, like I said. You could probably get hold of him there. His sister lives in Oakland. She was the youngest of them, just barely three. And listen, Mom says the other parents didn't have much to do with Brenda afterward. She doesn't know the details, I guess they didn't talk about it much because of Rachel dying, but Mom said she was—what's that word?—a *pariah* in the neighborhood after that."

"What's a pariah, Charlie? Brenda Wright was one after the kidnapping."

"An outcast. See if she knows who could tell us why."

"Do you know anyone who could tell us why she was an outcast after the kidnapping?"

Jill sounded smug. "I knew you were going to ask that, so I asked Mom. She said you should talk to Lucinda Todd."

"Who's she?"

"She was the Wrights' neighbor, and I guess she was a good friend of Brenda's, up until Rachel was killed. Mom said she'll talk your ear off. She still lives there. It's the house on the corner, right next to the Wrights' old house. Do you know where it is?"

I told her I did. I didn't want to go back to 13th Street, not ever again, but after saying goodbye to Jill, I told Charlie what she had said and naturally he said, *"Okay, let's go."*

I checked my voice mail first. I had one call, from Jonathan. I was so relieved when I heard him say *Good morning, Sunshine* that I felt a little shaky as I listened to the rest of the message: *I don't know if I'll be over tonight. I've got court all day tomorrow so I need to get some sleep. I have to be there at eight. I'd better just go home after work.* I could tell he was smiling when he added, *I'll get more sleep at my own place.* He spoke rapidly after that, trying to beat the beep that would cut him off: *Not that I wouldn't rather stay awake with you. Listen, if you're upset about last night—the murder, I mean— page me and I'll call you as soon as I can. I should be there with you but— You know how it is when I'm in court. I need to keep my mind on my testimony or I'll blow it. And, listen, don't do anything . . . uh, just arrange for the reward, okay? Talk to your lawyer, DeSilva, whatever his name is. He can handle it. You don't need to get involved. Gotta go. Talk to you later.* He finished at a gallop, beating the beep by about half a second.

I put the phone down. "I had a message from Jonathan," I told Charlie.

"Is he still mad at you?"

"He doesn't seem to be, but that doesn't mean I'm not still mad at you. I think I should call my lawyer and have him figure out how to do the reward. I don't really know how to go about it."

When I inherited Tom's money I also got his lawyer and his stock broker and his accountant. At first they called me up and told me what they were doing with my money, but it didn't take them long to figure out I didn't know what they were talking about, so now they just send me reports every once in a while. I don't understand the reports, either.

Jonathan's pretty cool about the money. He looked at one of the reports once and said, "Wow, are you rich!" but he doesn't really seem to be very impressed by it. When we go out to eat or to a show or something like that, he pays, but if we do something expensive—like last month when he took some vacation time because I wanted him to go to Hawaii with me—I pay for it and he doesn't have any problem with that. He just says he's lucky to have a girlfriend who's loaded. I wished we'd stayed in Hawaii. Maybe Charlie wouldn't have known where to find me.

I called Fernando DeSilva, who always sounds happy to hear from me. Something to do with that big retainer, I think. He said the reward needed to be anonymous or I'd have people all over the country wanting me to offer rewards for all kinds of things. He asked how many people I'd mentioned it to and didn't seem too happy about Jill. I told him I'd ask her not to tell anyone. He said he'd contact the Wrights himself and impress upon them the necessity for anonymity. I disconnected, remembering when I first learned the word *anonymity*.

Only good thing ever came out of Watergate is that everyone in the country learned how to pronounce anonymity, Duke says, taking a hit off his joint. *That, and getting rid of Tricky Dick Nixon.*

What's it mean, Duke? Anna . . . anna . . .

Means no one gets to know who you are. Deep Throat was the most anonymous bastard there ever was. Nobody ever knew who he was.

Who was he?

Don't know. Duke laughs, choking on the smoke he's exhaling. *He was the guy who told these two* Washington Post *reporters about Watergate. Bob Woodward and Carl Bernstein. They blew the cover-up all to hell and gone, won a Pulitzer for public service in journalism. They wrote a book about it, too, and then it was made into a movie–* All The President's Men, *damn good movie, too, with Al Pacino and Robert Redford. Deep Throat told them to follow the money, and that's what they did, followed the money right to the White House.*

Why'd they call him that, Duke?

He laughs, and Lady says, *You just be careful what you say to her.*

It was a code name, a secret name. They named him after a movie called Deep Throat. *Had a woman named Linda Lovelace in it, and a guy named Harry Reems. Big guy,* Duke says, grinning, but I don't know why.

Can we watch it sometime? I ask and Duke laughs until he chokes, and Lady has that prissy look on her face again.

CHAPTER EIGHTEEN

Lucinda Todd was about the same age as Brenda Wright, but she had aged a lot more gracefully than her ex-friend had, at least I thought so when I first saw her. She was a tiny thing, barely five feet tall, and probably weighed ninety-five pounds with a rock in her shoe, as Duke would have said. Her white hair was perfectly cut in a Princess Di style, and she was wearing khaki pants and a dark green top that brought out the color of her green eyes, which I thought were made up just a little too heavily for working in the yard.

She stopped raking when we walked up to her, and said, "Darn leaves. Rake, rake, rake, and the next day they're back."

"Maybe the wind will come up and blow them into the neighbor's yard."

She laughed like that was the funniest thing she'd ever heard. Duke used to say it whenever he raked.

"Aren't selling anything, are you? No, of course not, too well dressed. Aren't the police, are you? Already talked to all the cops I feel like talking to. 'Did you hear anything?' 'Did you see anyone?' How many times do I have to tell them no? These young officers today . . ." Words finally failed her, I guess. She just shook her head.

"I'm not a cop—"

"Too well dressed to be a cop."

"—but I am here about the shooting. Well, not the shooting actually, but about Rachel Wright."

She shook her head, tsk-tsking. "That poor child. Aren't a newspaper reporter, are you? No, of course not."

"Too well dressed," I said, and she laughed again. "I'm putting up some money for a reward for information about Rachel's murder."

"Ah. Well, guess you're dressed right for that. Who does your hair? Let me guess. Monsieur Jacques, right?"

"Right."

"Knew it. Only one in town who knows how to cut hair."

"Does he do yours?"

"Can't afford his prices. My sister does mine. Retired now, worked for a shop in San Jose for years. Better than Jacques if you ask me."

"It's a really good cut."

"Thank you. What did you say your name is?"

I hadn't said. "Lizbet Lange."

"Lucinda Todd. Well, let's go inside. No point in standing out here giving the neighbors something else to talk about."

We went in through the open garage door, squeezing past a car and a big chest freezer, and then we went through a door that led past a laundry room and into the kitchen. A walk down a short hall took us into the living room. Lucinda talked the whole time, telling me about her arthritis. She also told me her husband, Luther, was gone but I didn't know for sure if she meant he had died or he had just gone to the store or something and I didn't ask. I couldn't have anyway because she never shut up long enough.

The whole living room would have fit in one corner of my

formal living room. It was crowded with dark wood furniture upholstered in deep blues and greens; houseplants and framed photographs covered all the flat surfaces. A lone ceramic jack-o'-lantern sat on top of the television.

Lucinda twirled the rod on the miniblinds so sunlight slanted in across the dark green carpet. I sat down on the couch. Charlie took the chair beside it, then stood up quickly when Lucinda headed toward it. She walked through him, something I had never seen happen before. Charlie looks solid to me, so it was really weird seeing her body pass through his. My eyes crossed, I think, and I felt a little queasy. Charlie winked at me. I smiled at him, but I think my smile was just a little shaky. Lucinda didn't seem to notice she'd walked through a ghost.

"That poor child," she said, sitting down and smoothing the legs of her khakis. "Such a sweetie, always such a good girl. Not like her brother. Now there was an FLK if I ever saw one."

"A what? FLK?"

"Funny Looking Kid. My son's a doctor. It's what doctors call them—not in front of the parents, of course. Kids who are just a little strange, a little off, nothing you can put your finger on really, just funny looking."

I'd thought Ryan was funny looking, too, but it seemed kind of rude to say it to someone. Jill's mother was right about Lucinda talking my ear off. She hardly stopped long enough to breathe.

"School wanted to put him in a special class but Brenda raised such a stink they kept him in the regular class. Said she wanted him with Rachel. A mistake if you ask me, a brother and sister in the same class, especially when Rachel was younger—skipped a grade, you know—and so smart and Ryan was always behind in everything, never seemed to be able to keep anything in his head. One day he'd know his times tables, next day you'd swear he'd never heard of multiplication. Brenda said Rachel would help him learn. She wanted Rachel to keep an eye on him, keep him out of trouble, is what I think. That's a lot to ask of a little girl, if you ask me. Real protective of him though, Rachel was."

"What kind of trouble did he get into?"

"Oh, little things, telling lies, taking some kid's toy and not understanding why he couldn't keep it, pestering other kids until they got so mad they'd starting fighting with him just to get rid of him. Got in more trouble as he got older, though—shoplifting, things like that. Had a way of doing anything anyone told him to. Other boys would tell him to do something wrong and he'd just do it. Steal things from a teacher's desk, things like that. Don't know the details, just what I heard around the neighborhood. Didn't talk to Brenda except when I had to, not after Halloween of 'seventy-three. Lizabeth, right? Short for Elizabeth?"

"Yes, but it's *Lizbet.*"

"Lizbet. Wonderful name, Elizabeth, so many possibilities. Liz, Lizzie, Beth, Bess, Betty, Betsy. So many choices. Don't think I've heard Lizbet before."

"It's what my parents called me."

"What is it you want to know?" She was rubbing her hands together, massaging the knuckles, which were red and swollen. The backs of her hands were ridged with blue veins. Her face was so carefully made up and her hair was so perfect that her hands seemed to belong to someone else, someone much older.

"Whatever you know. I just thought I should know as much about it as possible."

"It's your money, right? Well, why not? What do I know about it? Know it never should have happened. Know Brenda was a fool."

"Why?"

"Why? Taking four little ones out trick-or-treating, and just Rachel to help her, that's why. Ryan wouldn't have been any help, more of a hindrance, hyper as he was. You have children? No ring, I see. Not married?"

"No."

"Well, I can tell you that she should have known better than to take those little ones out by herself, no other adult with her. Oh, Rachel was there, but she was just a child herself, wasn't she? Pure wonder she didn't lose them all."

"Their parents must have thought it was okay."

"Oh no they didn't. I was supposed to go with her, me and my two kids. Tina and Timmy were ten and twelve then. All of us were going trick-or-treating together so there'd be the two of us to watch the little ones. The bigger kids didn't need much watching, except for Ryan. Bouncing off the walls half the time, that boy was. But two grownups for the four little ones, that would have been just fine."

Timmy and Tina Todd. Alliteration again. Mr. What's-His-Name-the-GED-Teacher would have been surprised that I even knew the word. "Why did you change your mind about going with her?"

"I didn't. *She* did. Came over here that afternoon, all in a huff with some story about Timmy picking on Ryan, saying she didn't want him near her precious son ever again. Came over here looking for a fight, is what she did, and I'll tell you she got one. We were good friends before that, real good friends, *best* friends. Neither of us had a job, home all day with our kids, so we'd work on our photo albums or watch the soaps together, maybe just sit around talking while the little ones played. My Trisha was just five months older than Brenda's Rebecca."

Timmy, Tina, and Trisha. What was it with these people? Didn't they know they had twenty-six letters to choose from?

"Don't know what got into her. Timmy was a good boy— doctor now, did I tell you that? Yes, I did, didn't I? And Tina's married to an accountant. Good kids both of them. Trisha, too. Not married yet, though. I don't know, maybe Timmy did pick on him, they were just kids. Kids are always picking on each other, aren't they? But she blew it way out of proportion, came storming over here, yelling about Timmy, calling him a brat. Shocked me at first, hurt my feelings, then I got mad and we ended up in a regular shouting match, calling each other names, accusing each other of being bad mothers. Never have understood what got into her. You can believe I didn't want to take the kids trick-or-treating with her, not after the way she treated me, but I never dreamed she'd go by herself. I never thought about telling the others I wasn't going with her. Assumed she'd let them know, but she didn't, and believe me they were plenty mad when they found out. Plus, she took them *east.*"

"East?"

"That way. Past the park." She jerked a thumb over her shoulder. "Hospital's there now but it was low income then, old houses, trashy apartments. Just a block and a half away, but it was a whole different world on the other side of the park back then. Run-down houses, apartments full of . . . Hispanics and African Americans, most of them on welfare. Lots of children, they all had three or four at least, just like stairsteps, bang, bang, bang, one after another. Another baby, another few dollars of welfare money to spend on beer and cigarettes, that's how they thought. They came *here* on Halloween, we didn't take our kids *there.*"

I suddenly didn't like Lucinda. I didn't like that pause and the sly look on her face, like she was trying to figure out how I'd react if she said the words she really wanted to say instead of *Hispanic* and *African American.*

"She wasn't over there when Rachel disappeared, was she? It happened on this street."

"Not more than a block away from home when Brenda noticed Rachel was gone. But who knows how long she was gone? Brenda said she couldn't have been gone more than a few minutes before she noticed, but she had those four little ones to keep an eye on. Even admitted she wasn't sure exactly when she saw Rachel last, said she and Ryan had gone off by themselves part of the time because the little kids walked too slow. Could have been someone who saw them when they were over there, over by those apartments, someone who followed them until he could grab Rachel. They spent a lot of time over there questioning people, the police did."

"So that's why the other parents were mad at her, because she took them to the apartments?"

"That, and because she didn't tell them I wasn't going with her. Alicia Fenton and Marcia Offenbach were pregnant, both of them ready to pop any minute or they'd've taken their kids out themselves. Neither of 'em ever would have sent their little ones out with only Brenda to watch them. Mary Brown, well, maybe she would have. That Holly of hers used to run pretty wild. Black, you know. African American." This time she made it sound like a dirty word. "Only ones in the neighborhood back then. *This* neighborhood. Most of them lived over on the other side of the park. But John Brown got himself hired on as a patrolman—that affirmative action stuff, you know—had enough money for a down payment, moved his family in here."

I waited for her to add "and there wasn't anything we could

do to stop him" but she didn't. Charlie suddenly said, *"Don't let her get to you."* I glanced at him, then took a longer look. He was standing in the doorway to the hall, leaning one shoulder against the doorjamb, ankles crossed, thumbs hooked in the pockets of his jeans, fingers splayed on his thighs. He looked sexy as anything. I felt myself blush, and looked away quickly.

Lucinda had asked me something. "I'm sorry?"

"What else do you want to know?"

"Oh. Well, I don't really know. Just anything."

"Well . . . Brenda." She sighed, shaking her head. "What can I tell you about Brenda? We were good friends, like I said. They moved into the house next door in 'seventy-one, just a couple months after we bought this place. This was a new subdivision then. I didn't really know her before that, kept to herself, didn't socialize much. The day after they moved in, I went over, took her some homemade cookies, figuring we might as well get to know each other better since we were going to be neighbors. She'd been crying, I could tell. I asked her what was wrong and she told me she just found out she was pregnant. Didn't want the baby. Told me so herself, that very day, first time I ever really talked to her. Even talked about . . . getting rid of it. Asked if I knew anyone. It was illegal then, abortion was."

"Roe versus Wade wasn't until nineteen seventy-three."

"'Seventy-three? Was it? Yes, I suppose it was. Two years too late for Brenda. Don't approve really, but . . . truth is, if I'd known anyone, I'd have given her the name, that's how upset she was about being pregnant. Desperate, really. I was pregnant again myself, six months along with Trisha and I wasn't all that thrilled when I found out I was having another one—my older two were half grown by then—but I didn't see how any woman could kill her own baby, but Brenda was frantic, just frantic. She kept saying she just couldn't go through it again. I thought she meant being pregnant, giving birth, all the misery and pain. Later on I wondered if it was because she was afraid she'd have another one like Ryan. That child just wore her out. Wasn't until after Rebecca was born that she told me about the other one."

She leaned toward me, hands pressed against her knees, elbows cocked, looking like she was going to share a bit of really juicy gossip. I noticed how thick her makeup was, how the skin of her neck didn't match the carefully colored skin of her face, how she had darkened the line of her jaw to draw attention away from the sagging skin beneath it. I suddenly thought of Hansel and Gretel in the witch's house.

I swallowed hard, then said, "The other one?"

"The other baby. A little girl."

"Her baby?"

"Of course, hers. Rachel and Ryan's little sister. Crib death. Sudden Infant Death Syndrome they call it now. Found her dead in her cradle, Brenda did, not more than two months old."

"How awful. That's so sad."

"Sad, yes. And she was scared to death it would happen to Rebecca, too. Plain drove herself crazy worrying about it. Had the baby in a crib right by her bed, barely slept nights, sat in a rocking chair by the crib, only sleep she got was when she dozed off accidentally. It was summertime when Rebecca was born, June. The older kids were home from school. Rachel was a good girl, responsible, she could have watched that baby for a while during the day so her mother could get some rest, but, no, Brenda wouldn't let her, said she needed to watch the baby herself. So she never got any rest, watching over that baby every waking minute and most of the night, too. Larry, too, she had him up at some ungodly hour of the morning, four in the morning or something, taking his turn watching the baby so she could get a few hours of sleep.

"I offered to sit by the crib while the baby was napping in the afternoon so she could get some rest, but she wouldn't let me. Said she had to do it herself. I don't know how Larry stood it, her being almost a basket case the whole time, that whole summer. Things got better in the fall. Seemed like once the baby got past the age the other one was when it died, she wasn't so scared about her dying. I remember right after school started, I went over there in the afternoon and she had the front door open, just the screen closed, and I could see her sound asleep on the couch, little Rebecca in the playpen, sound asleep, too. Almost knocked on the door to wake her up because I knew how she was about watching that baby while she was sleeping, but I thought how much Brenda needed some rest, so I didn't. Went back though, just about every ten minutes all afternoon I walked over there and peeked in the door and made sure I could see that baby's back rising and falling. Last time I went, Brenda was awake and I'll tell you, that long nap did her a world of good. She was laughing and playing with the baby. I told her she should take a nap every afternoon, it did her good, and she laughed and said maybe she would. And she did. Just about every day, she'd sleep after lunch, wouldn't wake up until time for Rachel and Ryan to come home. She'd sleep on the couch with little Rebecca in her playpen, playing with her toys if she was awake. Good baby, that Rebecca, entertained herself right from the start. Anyway, seemed to me like Brenda just finally relaxed about it, finally started to believe the baby wasn't going to die in her sleep after all."

"Well, I'm glad she—"

"Terrible mother in some ways. Obsessive. Wouldn't let the

kids out of her sight when they were home. Never let them go
over to someone's house to play, always had to invite their friends
to their house, like she didn't trust anyone else to keep an eye
on them. Didn't even leave the kids with Larry, not if she could
help it. It was like she didn't even trust him with them. Why
that man put up with her nonsense, I don't know. Worked hard
supporting them, and she wouldn't even hire a sitter so they
could go out once in a while. Always talked about how she
never had a babysitter for them. 'We never go anyplace we can't
take the kids,' that's what she always said, like it was something
to be proud of, like I was a bad mother because I hired Jenny
Wilson to watch my kids while we went out to dinner or down
to the American Legion Hall. 'I need to be with the children,'
that's what she was always saying. But it wasn't true. Oh, they
didn't get a sitter and go out at night but all she ever wanted to
do was get rid of Rachel and Ryan. Couldn't wait to get them
off to school in the morning, had them down at the bus stop ten
minutes early even in the rain. Got upset if they were sick and
she had to keep them home, acted like they were doing it on
purpose. Signed them up for everything—scouts, swimming les-
sons, dance classes for Rachel, soccer and karate for Ryan—not
that he was any good at any of that, clumsy boy, never seemed
to know where his body was, if you know what I mean, and
small for his age, always way too thin. School nurse used to
check up on him at lunch time, make sure he ate something.
Would have just wasted away if someone hadn't made him eat.
And Ryan never lasted too long in any of the groups. She'd sign
him up and he'd go a few times, then she'd take him out because
he caused trouble, didn't seem to know how to act in a group.
But she kept signing him up for after-school activities, Brenda
did, kept trying to find some place to send him. Seemed like she

just didn't like being around them, and signing them up for those things was a way she could get them off her hands and still look like she was Mother of the Year."

"She still had Rebecca to take care of. Maybe she was—"

"And that's another thing. Favored Rebecca over the other two something awful. Precious little Rebecca. Spoiled her rotten, if you ask me. Big age difference, of course, those other two were half grown when Rebecca came along. Same with my kids, Trisha was a big surprise, never thought I'd have another, but I never spoiled her, never let Luther spoil her either."

"I suppose if she was so worried about crib death, she probably—"

"Guilt is what I think it was. She didn't want that baby, wanted to get rid of her before she was born. Felt so guilty about it she spoiled her rotten."

With a best friend like Lucinda, Brenda sure hadn't needed any enemies.

I folded my hands together in my lap and looked at them while I talked to Charlie. *"Are we through?"*

"See what she knows about Brad Hatcher."

"You must have known Brad Hatcher," I said to Lucinda.

"Him! Good riddance to bad rubbish."

"You didn't like him?"

"Couldn't stand the man. Brenda's brother, guess you know that. Regular slumlord now, owns three or four houses in the neighborhood, didn't keep them up like he should have. Brenda and Larry sold their house to him after Ryan got out of high school. He was in some kind of special ed class by then. All Brenda's carrying on couldn't keep him in regular classes any longer. She even tried home-schooling him for a while. Gave that up as a lost cause. Funny how he was. Talked good, you'd never know from listening to him that he could barely read. Seemed bright enough when you talked to him. Just couldn't keep anything in his head for more than a minute. Brenda about wore herself out tutoring him and it didn't do any good at all."

"What was wrong with Brad Hatcher?"

"Well, his wife was a slut for starters, used to be men over there when he was at work. The kids weren't too bad, stayed out of my yard anyway, but they were all in trouble by the time they were in high school. The girl was sleeping around, used to see her parked out front in some boy's car, windows so steamed up you couldn't see inside it."

I bet that had made her mad, them steaming the windows up so she couldn't watch what they were doing. I wondered if she owned a pair of binoculars.

"Both his boys were in trouble with the law, and him a cop himself. Drugs mostly, is what I heard. I didn't socialize with them. Hardly said two words to Paula Hatcher the whole time they lived there and that was close to fifteen years. Luther didn't get along with Brad at all. Partnered with him for a while, but couldn't stand him and asked for a different partner."

Good grief, *another* cop! I didn't want him telling Sterling I'd been here. I remembered her saying he was gone now; I thought about crossing my fingers that she meant he was dead, but that seemed pretty mean.

Lucinda was still rattling on: "Can't think when they moved out, early 'nineties, must have been. Kids were all grown by then. Sure wish they'd sold the house. Nothing worse than renters to ruin a neighborhood. Don't keep the yard up, just let it go to seed, dandelions all over the place, loud music blaring all the time, broken down cars on the street. Every time a renter moved out, he'd be over there painting the place, didn't matter if they were only there a few months, they managed to trash the place. Must be two dozen coats of paint on those walls by now. Seems like he couldn't keep a tenant, either. Someone new always moving in. Rented to Hispanics and blacks, too. Don't know how that kind come up with the money. Rent's not cheap in this neighborhood."

I stood up. "Well, thank you for taking the time to talk to me. I really need to leave now."

She looked surprised, like she'd just gotten started. She probably had, but I was sick of listening to her.

Charlie said, *"Ask her–"*

"I don't want to ask her anything. I'm leaving."

"Just ask her if she was home last night."

I asked her. She said, "I was at my daughter's house, didn't get home until after ten. Luther's not well, doesn't leave the house much anymore. He tires real easy and he fell asleep in front of the television. He didn't hear the gunshot but the sirens woke him up and he went over there to see what was going on."

I thanked her but I didn't say it was nice to meet her. The doorknob turned just as I touched it, making me jump. The man who opened the door looked as surprised as I felt.

"Luther, this is Lizbet Lange. She's putting up a reward for Rachel Wright's killer." Turning to me, she added, "Luther was a sergeant then, in charge of the investigation."

Luther looked about sixty. He had to be retired so maybe he wouldn't say anything to Sterling. He was tall and broad-shouldered but looked too thin, gaunt, like he'd been much heavier but had lost a lot of weight. His hair was gray and thin and he had dark circles beneath his eyes. He shook my hand, saying, "I wasn't really in charge, Lieutenant Cranston was. Sad case. That billboard, though, I don't know. It was Chief Sterling's idea, but

I don't expect anything to come of it. Whoever did it probably left the area back then, high-tailed it right out of here, and if anyone knew anything, why would they come forward now?"

"Maybe the reward will help."

"Well, yeah, money can be motivating, but still . . . it's been a long time. More likely, the department will be swamped with useless information from people who are after the reward."

"Are you still with the police?" I asked.

"Retired eleven years ago. I put in twenty-five years then took the pension."

"And went out and got another job," Lucinda said. "Try living on a cop's pension!"

"I worked security for a few years. I'd still be doing it but . . . my health's not too good."

He and his wife exchanged a look, and I suddenly knew that he was dying. His hand had felt too warm when I shook it, feverish almost. "Well, I really need to be going."

"Nice meeting you, Elizabeth. We'll be keeping our fingers crossed that your reward works, won't we, Lucinda?"

"Sure will."

I thought about saying it was Lizbet, not Elizabeth, but it didn't seem worth the effort. "I'll keep my fingers crossed, too," I said.

CHAPTER NINETEEN

I had parallel-parked the Porsche in front of my Volvo, which was right in front of Brad Hatcher's rental house. While we were walking across Lucinda's yard to the sidewalk, I said, *"Too bad you can't drive, Charlie."*

"I can drive."

"Yeah, but only a ghost car, right? I'd still have to get the real car home." I looked at Brad Hatcher's house, feeling myself shiver just at the sight of it. I thought there might be a strip of yellow police tape across the door, but there wasn't. They'd probably been there half the night, lifting fingerprints and stuff like that. At least I hadn't touched anything. Except the light switch in the kitchen. And the murder weapon.

We were almost to the Porsche when I stopped suddenly, staring past it at the Volvo. "Oh, god, *my car!* Look what someone did to my car!" I ran to the Volvo. The passenger side window was smashed, glittery chunks of the glass on the curb and pavement, the rest of it in the car, sprinkled across the seat and floor. *They throw a spark plug against the glass to shatter it, works every time:* Jonathan, telling me how car thieves work.

"Somebody broke into my car!" I ran around to the driver's door, pulling my key chain out of my purse and using the little gizmo that unlocks the doors. I opened the door and looked inside. The CD player was still there. There wasn't anything else in it to steal. I'd heard about people stealing airbags because you have to replace them every time they inflate so there's a big demand for them, but there was no sign of anyone messing with the airbags.

"Anything missing?" Charlie asked, sounding real calm, like having someone break into my car wasn't a big deal at all.

"They broke the window!"

"Check the glove box."

"I don't keep anything in there, just the papers and a flashlight."

"See if the registration's there."

"I wonder why they didn't take the CD player." I was leaning into the car, one knee on the seat. "Look, even the CDs are still here. They must've been scared off."

"See if the registration's there."

"Oh, for pete's sake, nobody would—" I backed out of the car, straightening up and looking at Charlie, my stomach doing funny flip-flops. "Oh, god. My address is on it. Oh, god. Somebody wanted to find out where I live." I scrambled into the front seat and reached over, opening the glove box. The flashlight was there. No papers. No insurance card. No registration. "Oh, god."

Charlie was leaning down, looking in the window at me. *"You need to stop talking to me. Luther Todd's standing at the door, watching you."*

"I don't care." I looked at the Todds' house; the door was just closing. So what if he thought I was nuts. I clenched my hands on the steering wheel and let my forehead drop against it, closing my eyes, seeing it all in my mind: a man in dark clothes, a fast flick of his wrist, a spark plug striking the window, glass shattering, the man leaning in, opening the glove box, grabbing the papers, running. Would the alarm go off? I wasn't sure. An impact would set it off but I wasn't sure breaking the glass would do it. It wouldn't matter anyway. It had to have happened in the middle of the night, after the cops left. He'd be gone by the time anyone got up to see whose car alarm was going off *this* time. Anyone who bothered to look outside would see nothing but dark cars parked at the curb, and before they got mad enough to call the cops, the alarm would stop, and they'd go back to bed. Maybe someone noticed the broken window this morning, but so what? It wasn't *their* car, and it was too late to do anything about it. They'd shrug, thinking the owner would take care of it and, besides, anyone who could afford a Volvo deserved it anyway.

I sat up straight and dug my cell phone out of my purse and called Jonathan's pager, saying "Oh, shut up" to the recording that was telling me to please press the buttons on my touchtone telephone as I wanted the number to appear on the pager. Why didn't Jonathan record his own message so I didn't have to listen to that stupid voice every time? I punched in my cell phone number. "He's in court. He won't be able to call until there's a break. What am I going to do?"

"Call Sterling."

"I don't know the number."

"Call nine-one-one."

They didn't have nine-one-one when Charlie was alive. So how did he know about it? Sometimes I suspect he knows everything—who kidnapped Rachel, who shot Brad Hatcher, who broke into my car. He probably knows who Deep Throat was. He told me in April that there had to be an "earthly explanation" for everything that happened. Nothing could happen that I couldn't explain, and that I couldn't understand once he went away and I forgot about him.

"Nine-one-one's only for emergencies. They don't like you calling it unless you're getting killed." This time after the stupid recording for Jonathan's pager shut up, I tapped in my cell phone number and added nine-one-one after it.

My phone rang barely a minute later. I didn't have a chance to say hello. As soon as I put the phone to my ear, I heard Jonathan say, "Where are you? What's wrong?" He was talking low, not quite whispering. In the background I could hear a man's deep voice droning on and on. A lawyer.

"Jonathan, someone . . ." I couldn't talk anymore because I started crying.

"You're scaring me. Where are you?"

"Thirteenth . . ." I drew a big shaky breath and held it for a second, then I said, "Thirteenth Street, where I was last night. Someone broke into the Volvo and stole the registration."

"You're okay? You're not hurt?"

"No, I'm okay. But, Jonathan, they took the registration."

I could almost feel him thinking, figuring it out. Cops are good at seeing all the possibilities when there's a crime involved. "Damn, why did I let you leave it there? You need to get hold of Sterling."

"I don't want to talk to him."

"Call him anyway. Look, I haven't testified yet but I think this thing's going to drag on another day. I'll see if I can leave. Stay there, okay? I'll be on my way as soon as I can. Leave your phone on. I'll call back if I can't come. And call Sterling."

"Okay." I added "Hurry!" but he'd already hung up.

I didn't want to call Sterling. I wanted Jonathan. Charlie was in the passenger seat. I hadn't noticed when—or how—he'd gotten in the car. He was sitting on cracked safety glass, unless he'd brushed it off. It wouldn't matter to him, anyway; he was just a ghost. "I wish you were real," I said. *So you could hug me,* I thought, *so I could put my head on your shoulder and you could put your arms around me and hold me tight and tell me everything is going to be all right.* Charlie smiled and said, *"So do I."*

We just sat there for a long time, not talking, then Charlie said, *"You really should call Sterling."*

I called Information and asked for the number of the Oak Valley Police, then I called that number and asked for Chief Sterling. "Tell him it's Lizbet Lange," I told the bored-sounding man who had answered. "Tell him it's important."

"One moment, please." I was put on hold. At least they didn't play any music. After a minute of silence, another woman said, "Chief Sterling's office. May I help you?" His secretary; I recognized her voice.

"This is Lizbet Lange. Put Sterling on."

She didn't say anything for a moment. I pictured her taking the phone away from her ear and looking into the little holes in the receiver like she could see who the rude person on the other end was. "Your name again?"

"Lizbet Lange. Just put him on, okay?"

"One moment, please." And this time I got music, an instrumental version of a song Lady used to play all the time. I grew up listening to Duke and Lady's music from the 'sixties and 'seventies but I was too upset to think of the words.

"Ms. Lange?"

"Somebody smashed my car window."

"I see." He sounded like he was smiling. "Well, most people don't report broken windows directly to the chief of police but I'm sure your insurance—"

"The *Volvo*! Someone broke into the Volvo! On Thirteenth Street! I left it here. Someone smashed the window and the registration's gone!"

Sterling didn't say anything for a moment. "The registration's gone?"

"Yes! My address is on it, someone wanted my address!"

"Are you on Thirteenth Street right now?"

"*Yes*, that's where the car is." *Idiot!*

"Stay there." He hung up.

I stayed there, crossing my arms on the top of the steering wheel and resting my forehead on them, thinking about the song on the telephone. I remembered what it was now: "Killing Me Softly With His Song," Roberta Flack's Grammy winner from 1973, which was still the 'sixties, not the 'seventies, at least that's what Duke always said.

When people talk about the 'sixties, Duke says, *they don't mean nineteen sixty. That was still the 'fifties. Hell, Ike was still president in nineteen sixty. Kennedy took over in January of 'sixty-one, but the 'sixties didn't really start until 'sixty-three, when the Beatles had their first hit single in the U. S. of A.—"She Loves You."*

Yeah, yeah, yeah, I say, and Duke cracks up laughing.

The Beatles broke up, I tell him, and he nods sadly, saying, *Yeah, they performed together for the last time in nineteen seventy. But the 'sixties didn't end then. It was still the 'sixties until* Saturday Night Fever—*that's a movie, Lizzie-Lou, came out in 'seventy-seven. Had John Travolta in it. Disco music. That's what ended the 'sixties, disco and punk rock. It wasn't the same after the Beatles broke up, but there was some good music in the early 'seventies.*

*Nineteen seventy-*three, *Duke. You were telling me about nineteen seventy-three.*

"Seventy-three? Well, let's see. Roberta Flack won the Grammy for best record for a song called "Killing Me Softly With His Song," second year in a row she won it. She got it for "The First Time Ever I Saw Your Face" in 'seventy-two. Stevie Wonder got the Best Album Grammy for "Innervisions." He doubled up, too; got another Grammy in 'seventy-four. 'Seventy-three . . .

There were a lot of good songs that year, Lady says. *"You're So Vain," "Midnight Train to Georgia," "You Are the Sunshine of My Life."*

Stevie Wonder, I say. I like that one. Duke sings it to me sometimes.

Jim Croce's "Time in a Bottle" was released posthumously, Lady says. *That means it came out after he died, Lizbet. He was killed in a plane crash that year. Bobby Darin died in 'seventy-three, too, of a heart attack.*

Duke snorts. *Only good song Croce did was "Bad, Bad Leroy Brown."* He stares off into space, slowing exhaling smoke, his eyes half-closed. *'Seventy-three. 'Seventy-three was the beginning of the end.* He seems to be watching the smoke drifting off the joint he's holding between his thumb and index finger.

Behind the screen door, Lady says, *The war ended in 'seventy-three.*

Duke glances up, looking at her like he doesn't know what she's talking about, or maybe like *she* doesn't know what she's talking about. With a dismissive wave of his hand he says, *Yeah, the war ended. Vietnam War, Lizzie-Bet. The cease-fire went into effect on the twenty-eighth of January. By the end of March all the US troops were home.*

Except the MIA's, Lady says, touching the silver band on her wrist, a bracelet engraved with the name of a soldier missing in action.

The prisoners of war were all released on the first of April. Came home from serving their country just in time to watch it all fall apart, just in time for Watergate.

Supper's about ready, Lady says, and I hurry inside. I've heard Watergate before, and I know it's a long, long story.

CHAPTER TWENTY

Chief Sterling arrived in an unmarked car with a flashing blue bubble light on the dash. I saw Lucinda peeking out her miniblinds as he parked in Brad Hatcher's driveway. I got out of the car and he walked over to me and we stood by the Volvo, staring at the broken window like maybe it would do something interesting.

"Think back. You said you didn't see anyone. Are you sure?"

"Positive."

"The newspaper didn't mention you by name, just said Hatcher's body was found by a visitor who arrived shortly after the shooting. Same with the news on television."

"That's why they stole my address."

"But how would anyone know your car had anything to do with it?"

"Well . . . it doesn't belong here. Maybe it was someone in the neighborhood who knows the car doesn't belong to anyone who lives around here."

"We don't have any reason to suspect any of the neighbors. You're positive you didn't see anyone, no one walking past when you drove up, no jogger running down the sidewalk, no car pulling away when you got here?"

"No. I didn't see anyone. Well, I saw a car pull up over there."

I pointed to an empty spot down the street. "There was a minivan parked in front of that house and a car came and parked behind it but no one got out. I thought it was kids parking but later I thought it must have been Detective Flynn."

"It was."

"I never went near my car again. One of the cops drove me to the police station."

"And you didn't see anyone."

How many times was he going to ask that? "*No*, I didn't see anyone. They kept asking me that last night. I told them I didn't see anyone." I chewed on my lip and stared at the broken window. "Well, there was that man across the street."

Chief Sterling had been looking at Hatcher's house. He turned slowly and stared at me. He sighed. I knew he would. "Tell me about this man."

"He was at that house on the corner." I pointed to it, noticing for the first time that there was a sign on the lawn. "The one that's for sale," I said. "And he walked across the lawn and got in a car and it took off."

"The house isn't for sale, it's for rent."

"Well, whatever."

"It's another of Brad Hatcher's rentals."

"Oh."

"What did this man look like?"

"I don't know. It was dark."

"Try to remember."

How was I supposed to remember something I didn't know? "He was just a man."

"White? Black?"

"Um . . . white, I guess. It was dark. I didn't see his face. He was just a man."

"The dome light would have come on when he opened the door."

I thought about that for a minute. "I don't think it did."

"No dome light. So he walked across the yard, got in the car, and drove off."

"Yes. Well, actually, he sort of stopped for a minute, in the middle of the lawn, not a minute, a couple seconds. I thought maybe he saw me and was wondering what I was doing."

Sterling made a sound in his throat, sort of a growl but not at all like Jonathan's sexy growl. "You told us you didn't see anyone."

"I forgot about him. I was upset. There was all that blood . . ." I looked all around, at the Volvo, the Porsche, Hatcher's house, Sterling's car in the driveway, the empty place where the minivan and Detective Flynn's cars had been parked, Lucinda's front window. I could see her fingers holding down one of the slats on the miniblinds so she could get a better look. I didn't want to look at Sterling so I looked at Charlie, who said, *"Better tell him, whatever it is."*

A psychic ghost. Just what everyone needs.

Without looking at Sterling, I said, "He wasn't driving the car."

"What?"

"He got in the passenger side and then whoever was driving it drove off."

Sterling turned away suddenly, walking quickly over to his car, then spinning on his heel and walking back to me, using up the energy that he really wanted to use to smack me. He stood with his hands on his hips, his jacket pushed back, his holster showing. "Someone was sitting in a car the whole time you were here, watching you, and you just now remember to tell me?"

"I forgot about it. I never thought about it having anything to do with . . ."

"The murder."

The word made my insides ache. The murder. The murderer. Oh, god, what if he was the murderer, what if the murderer was watching me, watching me get out of my car, watching me stand by the door, watching me go inside. Watching me watching him walk across the lawn and get in a car. What if he thought I could identify him?

Sterling had said something. "What?"

"Describe the car."

"It was just a car. I didn't pay any attention to it."

"Old, new, dark, light. You have to remember something."

"Not old. Not real old anyway. It was . . . it had round bumpers, not real bumpers like old cars. It was . . . dark colored. Not white, anyway."

"Not too old and not white. I don't suppose there's a hope in hell that you noticed the license plate."

I didn't bother answering.

"Think about the man again. How would you describe him? Tall and skinny, short and fat?"

"Neither. He was just a man. Not real skinny, but he wasn't fat either. His clothes were dark."

"All right. Keep thinking about it. If you remember anything else, get hold of me right away. I'm going to follow you to your house, make sure you get inside safely. You need to stay there."

"Jonathan's on his way. You don't need to follow me home."

He looked from the Volvo to the Porsche and back again. "How were you planning on getting home?"

"When? Now? I was going to drive, of course."

"Both cars?"

Uh-oh.

"What are you doing here if you didn't come to pick up your car?"

"Um . . ." I felt a good lie coming on, but it was too late. Lucinda and Luther were on the way.

Chapter Twenty-one

While Sterling was saying hello to the Todds, Jonathan arrived, double-parking his car by the Porsche and running to me, hugging me hard. I pressed my face into the curve where his neck met his shoulder. Lucinda was telling Sterling that I had been asking her about Rachel Wright. Sterling was trying to be polite, asking Luther how he was doing and all that, but I could feel his anger even though I wasn't looking at him; it was coming off him in waves, scorching me, making my face burn.

After telling the Todds goodbye, all he said was "My office. *Now.*" I think he was talking to Jonathan, not me. I heard him walk away and then a car door slammed and an engine started. He peeled rubber backing out of the driveway and again when he took off down the street.

Jonathan said, "What was that all about? What's going on?"

I raised my head. "You'll get mad at me, too."

"No I won't."

"Yes you will."

"No I won't."

I told him. He didn't get mad, not at first; he got confused.

He asked me why on earth I was running around town asking people about Rachel Wright. When I couldn't come up with a good explanation, I got a lecture. He kept it up as we drove to the police station. In *his* car. Now I had two cars parked on 13th

Street. Pretty soon they'd start charging me for parking. By the time we got to the police department, Jonathan had got himself worked up enough that he *was* mad, demanding to know just what the *hell* I thought I was doing questioning people about a murder. The reason was in the back seat. Without turning around to look at him, I said, *"I'd kill you if you weren't already dead, Charlie."*

Charlie ignored me. I ignored Jonathan, especially after he said, "Who do you think you are? Lizbet Lange, Girl Sleuth? There's a *killer* out there. Jesus. My timing may suck but you don't have a brain in your head."

I decided I was going to take all my money out of the bank and go someplace very far away, where no one could find me, not Jonathan, not Sterling, and not Charlie, although I wasn't too sure I could get away from *him*. I could send him away, though. I did it in April and he couldn't come back until I called him. But what good would that do? It wouldn't change what had already happened. I'd still be in the same mess, and I wouldn't have Charlie to help me figure it out. Not that he'd ever been all that much help, but at least he knew why I was doing what I was doing. It would be worse if I sent him away and forgot about him. Then even *I* wouldn't know why I was doing what I was doing.

Sterling started out by telling Jonathan he had to babysit me. That isn't the word he used, but that's what he meant.

"I'll be in court again all day tomorrow."

Sterling swore.

I was suddenly madder than I was scared. I headed toward the door. "I'm going home."

Jonathan and Sterling both said, "No you aren't."

"Yes I am." I had my hand on the doorknob when Charlie said, *"Stay and see what he can tell us."*

"Ms. Lange, you seem to be missing the point. You might have seen the killer. Worse, the killer might have seen you."

The things I do for Charlie. I took a seat in front of Sterling's desk. Jonathan moved behind me, resting his hands lightly on my shoulders. I shrugged them off.

"Maybe he wasn't the killer," I said.

"He was coming out of a vacant house, a house owned by Brad Hatcher."

"I didn't actually see him come out of the house, I just saw him walk across the yard. Maybe he was looking at the house, maybe he was thinking about renting it and he was looking in the windows, trying to see what it was like inside. Besides, if he was the killer and he just shot someone, why would he go over there, why didn't he leave? Wasn't he afraid the cops would show up?"

"Only one person reported the first shot and I'm kind of surprised anyone did. It was fired inside a building and it was cool enough last night that people probably had their windows closed. A single gunshot attracts less attention than you'd think. Most people assume it's a car backfiring and when nothing else exciting happens, they forget about it. Dispatch logged two calls about your gunshot, but it was the *second* shot that got people's attention a lot more than the first one. But you're right; I can't think of any reason he'd go there. Maybe he *was* just looking at the house. I sent a unit over. They're going to question the neighbors again; maybe someone else saw him. Maybe someone saw him break into your car and didn't bother reporting it. If that was the killer, he has your name and address."

I nodded, feeling ice cold and sick to my stomach. Then I said, "Oh."

"'Oh,' what?" Sterling said.

"I just remembered. It doesn't matter about the registration because it doesn't have my address on it. When the lawyer transferred the title or whatever, I hadn't made up my mind yet whether I was going to live in Tom's house or sell it, so he put my old address on it, where I was living then. I was supposed to change it, but I never got around to it."

Charlie was grinning, enjoying the look Jonathan and Sterling were exchanging. I could almost hear them thinking, *"Women!"*

Sterling said, "So he just has your name. I assume your phone's unlisted."

"It is," Jonathan said, "and you don't need to worry about him going after the wrong person at her old apartment in San Jose. It's vacant now. They're tearing it down to make a parking lot."

"Well, then," Sterling said, "it appears that we don't need to be overly concerned about your safety, Ms. Lange. But I still want you to stay home and stop talking to people about Rachel Wright. If you talk to the wrong person, if someone starts to worry that you know something you shouldn't, well, it wouldn't be all that hard to follow you home, would it? Here," he said, handing me a paper covered with single-spaced typing. At the top it said: Report Summary and it was dated October 31, 1973.

I must have looked surprised. He shrugged, saying, "You might as well know the facts." Charlie took the paper, a ghost copy that separated from it, leaving the real paper in my hand. I knew that if I looked at his ghost paper, I'd be able to see the words on it, but I wouldn't be able to comprehend them. Jonathan sank down on his heels beside my chair; I tipped the page a little so he could read it with me.

By six-twenty, the four little children had been dropped off at the Wrights' house so Brenda could take them trick-or-treating. The other parents all believed that Brenda's friend, Lucinda Todd, and her two kids were joining the group. Brenda didn't tell them she'd had a fight with Lucinda and was taking the kids out alone. She said she didn't want to inconvenience the other parents and she knew she could handle the four little ones with Rachel to help her.

At six-thirty, Brenda, Ryan, Rachel, and the four little kids went out trick-or-treating. Brad Hatcher was at the house with little Rebecca. Larry Wright arrived home at about six-forty and took over the candy-dispensing and babysitting responsibilities from his brother-in-law, who went upstairs.

The plan was for Brenda to walk the kids a block or two south on 13th Street, letting them trick-or-treat at the houses on the east side of the street, then cross the street and head back the way they'd come, stopping at the houses on the west side of the street. Two blocks north of the Wrights' house, they'd drop Tony and Sandy Fenton and Holly Brown off at their homes, then the remainder of the group would walk north one more block to take Billy Offenbach home, then Brenda, Ryan, and Rachel would walk back to their house, trick-or-treating on the east side of the street on the way.

That was the plan. But you know what they say about best-laid plans.

Instead of following the planned route, Brenda took the kids to the park a block behind her house, where the Parks Department had turned a large tent into a haunted house. Brenda waited outside with the little ones while the two older kids went inside. Realizing the stop at the haunted house had seriously cut into their trick-or-treating time, Brenda decided to take the kids to the apartment buildings just past the park, where they could collect more candy faster because there were so many units, so many doors so close together. The whole area was swarming with trick-or-treaters and she felt it was perfectly safe. After that, they walked back through the park and were on 13th Street, one block north of the Wrights' house, when Brenda realized Rachel wasn't with them. She went to the nearest house and asked the people there to call the police. Officer John Sterling arrived on the scene at seven twenty-five. The rest of the report explained where the cops searched that night. The last line was "The child was not located." There must have been other pages to the report, but that was all Sterling had given me.

"You were there," I said when I finished reading.

"I was there. I was the first cop on the scene. I'd been a cop for five years. I'd responded to reports of missing children plenty of times; they always turned up safe, except for a few cases that involved custody disputes. But Rachel didn't. The case has haunted me for over a quarter of a century."

When Sterling said "haunted" I looked at Charlie, who winked at me. He was standing beside Jonathan. They could have been identical twins. Well, almost. Jonathan's hair was a couple shades darker and much shorter, and he was just a smidgen taller, but that might have been because he was wearing dress shoes and his father was wearing sandals. Jonathan was wearing his testi-fying-in-court outfit: gray suit, white shirt, gray tie with a tiny pattern that I knew was handcuffs up close; Charlie was in his undercover-cop hippie clothes, of course. But they were still enough alike to take my breath away. It occurred to me that Jonathan was going to get older and older but his father was never going to age at all. I realized I was looking from one to the other, back and forth, and that Jonathan had noticed. He glanced to his left, where, to him, there was nothing, but, to me, there was his father. "What is it?" he asked.

"Nothing, nothing at all . . . The case haunted you," I said to Sterling, prompting him to go on. He'd been watching me, too, eyebrows raised, and I wondered what expression had been on my face while I was looking at Charlie and Jonathan, my two cops, one living, one dead. Sterling didn't know what *haunted* meant.

"When I arrived on the scene," Sterling said, "Brenda Wright was hysterical. I hadn't been around her much but there was a lot of talk around the department that she was high-strung and a very over-protective mother. Whenever a bunch of us and our wives would get together, Larry would come alone, said Brenda didn't like to leave the kids with a sitter. So, I figured she was over-reacting. Hell, half the people in the neighborhood were walking around trick-or-treating, the other half were at their front doors most of the time, handing out candy. What I mean is, it wasn't a lonely, deserted place. It was hard to imagine anyone snatching a kid with that many people around. And Rachel was *ten*, not two or three. I figured she'd show up. Larry thought so, too. I'd sent someone to the house to get him and after he calmed his wife down a little, he drove around the neighborhood, looking for the girl. Brad Hatcher went out in his car looking for her, too."

Jonathan said "Christ!" softly. I didn't understand why.

Sterling was looking at Jonathan, his chin jutting out defensively. "You have to understand: they were cops, guys I knew, guys I worked with, guys I went drinking with. Hell, guys I trusted to cover my back. And Hatcher and Wright had been with the department longer than I had. We were beat cops, all three of us, but in terms of seniority they both outranked me."

"Oh!" The light had dawned. "You think one of them did it! Rachel could have been in one of their cars. But why would either of them kill Rachel?"

"To protect himself is the only motive I've ever come up with."

"Protect himself? From Rachel? What could she do to him, to either of them?"

"She could tell."

I felt goosebumps rise on my arms. Telling is the one power children have; they use it against each other all the time.

I'm going to tell, I'm going to te-ell.

Don't tell, please don't tell.

You can't ever tell.

Promise me you won't tell.

You better not tell.

I'll kill you if you tell.

I'm going to tell, I'm going to te-ell.

"It said she wasn't raped or anything in the paper."

"There wasn't any physical evidence of sexual assault, none at all. But maybe he didn't do anything to her, maybe he forced her to do things to him, oral sex, for example, and unless it happened shortly before she was killed, there'd be no evidence. Maybe it wasn't even that bad, maybe he exposed himself, or asked her to take off her clothes, or just touched her. Who knows? It's the only motive I've ever come up with. It's a powerful motive. It's a secret no one wants told."

Don't you ever tell anyone what I did.

I won't tell, I promise, I promise.

I'll kill you if you tell.

But if a grownup really wanted his secret kept, he would kill you before you could tell.

"Which one do you think it was?" I thought of Larry Wright, who would make a good Santa and who looked so sad when he talked about Rachel. "Not her father."

"No, I think it was Brad Hatcher, the uncle who moved in with them a month before, whose marriage was on the rocks, who was known to drink a little too much and a little too often, who wasn't getting any from his wife so maybe his cute little niece started looking good to him after a few drinks."

"God, that's sick." I reached out to Jonathan and he took my hand.

"Yeah, it's sick. But it happens. Whoever killed Rachel managed to do it within a very narrow time frame. It was less than an hour from when they left the house to when Brenda asked the people down the street to call the cops. There's no way to know for sure how long the girl was gone before her mother noticed. Brenda didn't think she was missing for more than a few minutes, but she was busy watching the other kids, and Rachel and Ryan didn't stay with the group the whole time—the little kids were too slow so they kept going off on their own. But I can't see her being gone for more than ten or fifteen minutes without her mother noticing. So I figure he had about that long to grab the girl, kill her, and stash the body."

Jonathan said, "And then all the time in the world to take the body to a better hiding place because the cop who showed up to investigate let him get in his car and drive off."

"That's right, Dillon; I'm not denying it, although I don't get full blame for it. My sergeant had shown up by then and he was in charge."

"Another pal of Hatcher's," Jonathan said.

"Sure. We were all friends—we all knew each other, anyway—and we were cops. You know the drill: cops stick together.

Oak Valley was a small town then. I don't think there were more than twenty-five of us in the whole department."

"You definitely ruled out a stranger?" Jonathan asked.

"As much as it's possible to. When Rachel's body was examined, there wasn't a single fiber, a single hair, a single smudge of dirt that couldn't be traced back to her home or to the field where the body was found. The medical examiner said she wasn't in the field more than an hour. That was based on"—Sterling shot me a quick look, then continued with his voice lowered, like he thought I wouldn't hear—"insect, uh, activity. She was left in plain sight of the road; the first person who drove by after dawn reported it.

"The M.E. couldn't pinpoint the time of death, too much time passed before her body was recovered, but he said there was no way she was alive much past seven o'clock, seven-thirty at the latest. That was based on an analysis of stomach contents; she ate just before they left the house. She was reported missing at seven-twenty. The M.E. said time of death was no later than seven-thirty, so she was killed almost immediately. She wasn't sexually molested. She was just killed. Why would a stranger snatch a little girl and immediately kill her? Anyone who kidnaps a girl that age usually has some sort of sexual motive."

"Maybe she fought and he killed her trying to keep her quiet," I suggested.

"Could be, but there was no sign that she'd struggled, no marks on her other than the blow to the back of the neck."

"Any idea what was she hit with?" Jonathan asked.

"Something hard."

Was that supposed to be a joke? Sterling didn't look like he was trying to be funny.

"I thought he had an alibi," I said. "It said in the paper that Larry Wright and his brother-in-law were together."

"Wright said Hatcher was in the house the whole time, but he admitted he didn't actually see him for at least half an hour, maybe a little longer. They'd moved Ryan into Rachel's room with her while Hatcher was there, and he'd been staying in the boy's bedroom—upstairs. There's an outside stairway from the deck off the master bedroom. He could have left the house without being seen. Wright was in the living room, handing out candy to trick-or-treaters. He insisted he'd have heard Hatcher leave, but he had the television on and the little girl was with him, and she was fussy because she was sick, and there was a steady stream of trick-or-treaters. And Hatcher's car was parked around the corner. Nothing odd about that really; those houses all have one-car garages and it wasn't always easy to find a parking place on the street, not after people got home from work. It was convenient though, that being a day he had to park around the corner."

"Let's talk," Charlie suddenly said.

"Alone, you mean?"

"Yeah."

I stood up. "Excuse me. I need to use the bathroom."

"Here," Sterling said, rummaging in a desk drawer. He held out a key and pointed to a door in the wall to the right of his desk. "Second door on the right."

I took the key. "The police chief's executive restroom?"

"If you want to call it that. There won't be any drunks puking in it, anyway."

I looked at Charlie and said in my mind: *"My office. Now."* Charlie laughed.

CHAPTER TWENTY-TWO

The bathroom was tiny, and not far enough down the hall for me to feel safe talking out loud. I closed and locked the door and said, *"Okay, what is it?"*

"Brenda Wright was a block away from her house when she missed Rachel. What's the first thing you'd do if you suddenly realized your kid was missing?"

"Look for her."

"Look for her where?"

"Everywhere."

"First thing I'd do is see if she'd gone home."

"Oh, yeah."

"Brenda didn't. She went to a stranger's house and told them her daughter was missing and asked them to call the cops."

"You mean you think she knew Rachel couldn't be at home? He said she was hysterical. Maybe she just wasn't thinking. But you're right, Charlie. Even if she didn't think about Rachel going home, she would have wanted her husband, wouldn't she? She'd want to be with him, she'd at least want him to know Rachel was missing. But she couldn't have killed her, could she? What would she do with the body? Ryan was with her, and the little kids. I don't see how she could have done it. And why? Why would she kill her own daughter? Ryan sounds like the kind of kid you'd be likely to kill, not Rachel."

"Maybe she didn't. But her reaction seems all wrong to me."

"So . . . did you want me to kind of bring it up to Sterling?"

"Couldn't hurt."

I flushed the toilet and ran some water, just in case the sound carried. When we were back in the office, I said, "You know, it seems funny to me that Brenda didn't run home to see if Rachel was there. Wouldn't you think that's what she'd think of first? That Rachel had gone home?"

Sterling said, "She was hysterical."

"Still, wouldn't you think she'd check? I mean, why jump to the conclusion that she was kidnapped?"

"Mothers tend to panic when it comes to their kids."

"Well, I tried, Charlie."

"That's a good point, actually," Jonathan said. "It was only a block away, right? Seems to me she'd go get her husband. He was a cop, he'd know what to do. She should have at least sent the boy home to get him."

"I don't think she would have let him out of her sight right then; she already had one missing child. Besides, Ryan wasn't the kind of kid you sent on errands, not if you wanted them done right. He had a way of losing sight of what he was supposed to be doing. What I want, Ms. Lange, is for you to go home and stay there. Set your alarms. Don't open the door to anyone you don't know. Call me if anything odd happens, callers that hang up on you without talking, anything like that. I wish I had a picture of Larry and Brenda Wright so you'd know them if you saw them."

I must have looked guilty. Both Sterling and Jonathan stared at me for a moment, then Sterling said, "Don't tell me. You went to their house."

"I just wanted to talk to them about the reward."

"You've been busy, haven't you? What else have you done?"

"Nothing."

"You're sure? Come to think of it, how did you know Lucinda Todd knew about it? Did you knock on every door on Thirteenth Street?"

"Jill's mother said I should talk to her."

"Jill's mother. Ms. Lange, I'm trying to run an investigation here and you've got everybody and her mother sticking their noses into it. Go home, stay home. You see that she does, Dillon."

"I'll be with her until tomorrow morning. I can't get out of going to court."

"I don't need a babysitter. Do you really think Larry or Brenda Wright killed Brad Hatcher?" I asked.

"I think it's possible, if they finally suspected him of killing Rachel, although I don't know why they would after all these years. They said they were home together last night. Not much of an alibi, but one that's hard to disprove. None of the neighbors remember seeing them at all. If that was the killer you saw, and there was a second person in the car, which it sounds like there was, then maybe both of them went over there to confront him and one of them shot him. *Why now?* is the big question."

"The billboard brought it all back to them, made them start thinking about it again," Jonathan said. "Maybe one of them remembered something that pointed to Hatcher as the killer."

I said, "Maybe they were all talking about it and Brad Hatcher slipped up and said something wrong, something he wasn't supposed to know about."

Sterling looked like he was thinking that over. "What could it be? Hatcher's story was simple: he was upstairs the whole time. It's not like he had an elaborate alibi to remember."

"I don't know. I was just thinking out loud. What if . . . what if *Ryan* knew something that he'd never told? His parents have probably been talking about Rachel's murder a lot because of the billboard but it's probably the first time in years that they've even mentioned it. What if Ryan suddenly remembered something and told them? Maybe he suddenly figured out that his uncle molested Rachel. He was only ten, maybe he didn't even realize what he saw then, but maybe when he started thinking about it, he suddenly understood. You know, if he'd seen his uncle zipping up his pants or something. A ten-year-old might not get it."

"That's not a bad scenario," Sterling said. "Rachel's murder had to be premeditated, no way he could pull it off without planning it in advance. Maybe he knew Ryan saw something, maybe he was afraid if Ryan mentioned something to his parents Rachel might break down and tell them what was going on. With Rachel gone, there was no one to confirm anything Ryan said."

"Where was Ryan last night?" Jonathan asked.

"At work. Seven in the evening to three in the morning. He works at a warehouse and he's closely supervised. He never left." Sterling moved some papers around on his desk, not looking like he was even thinking about what he was doing. "This is all pure speculation. There's no solid evidence that Hatcher did it, it's just my gut feeling. It was a long time afterward before I even seriously thought about him. I knew him, after all. He passed a lie detector test. So did Wright. Brenda took one, too, but she broke down before they even got her hooked up. Her responses were so erratic they couldn't be analyzed.

The polygraphist said it looked like she was lying about everything, including her own name."

"Cops know how polygraphs work," Jonathan said. "I don't know if I could beat one, but I know how it's done."

"Sure. We all do. Hatcher's a bullshitter, too. Was, I mean. He was always bragging, taking some simple incident and blowing it up to make himself look good, make himself the big hero. He could make a routine traffic stop sound like a life-and-death situation."

"Pathological liar," Jonathan said.

"Maybe not technically, but he could lie like a sonofabitch, that's for sure."

Sterling and Jonathan started talking about me, wondering if it would be better if I stayed at Jonathan's apartment. I said "Absolutely not" to that because Jonathan had a temporary roommate, a cop whose wife had kicked him out, and I didn't feel like listening to him crying in his beer all the time. Besides, whoever broke into the car didn't get my address, so why worry?

Sterling had put the paper I'd read on top of a file folder. While they were going on and on about my alarm system, I opened the folder and looked at the top paper. Sterling noticed, and caught my eye for a second, but he didn't say anything. I realized I was looking at the autopsy report on Rachel Wright's body. I couldn't concentrate enough to really read it; words just jumped out at me, making me feel sick: Post mortem interval. Post mortem lividity. Degree of putrefaction. Gastric contents. Rachel's last meal was a tuna sandwich and potato chips. I let the cover of the file folder fall into place.

I promised Sterling I'd stay home the next day. But when I looked at Charlie, I knew I wouldn't. I also told him I was having a Halloween party the day after that. "At your house?" he asked.

"Well, of course. You can come if you want to. It starts at eight."

"I don't like Halloween, haven't liked it since nineteen seventy-three. But thanks for the invitation."

Not long after that, Jonathan and I left—and Charlie, of course. We went to 13th Street so I could drive the Porsche home. Jonathan had made a phone call from Sterling's office and a tow truck arrived right after we did. I thought towing the Volvo was a big waste of money but Jonathan said it was the easiest way to get it out of there and it had to go to the Volvo dealership anyway so they could replace the window, and it wasn't like I couldn't afford it. With Charlie in the passenger seat of the Porsche, I followed Jonathan up into the foothills.

"There are things that don't make sense," Charlie said.

Yeah, just about everything I'd done since he showed up. *"Like what?"* We were only a car-length behind Jonathan so I couldn't talk out loud in case he saw me chatting to thin air in his rearview mirror.

"Why hide the body somewhere for three days then drop it off where it would be sure to be found?" Charlie asked.

"I don't know. Don't call her it.*"*

"People usually refer to bodies as 'it.'*"*

"Well, I don't like it. So don't do it."

"It was an interesting plan, wasn't it? Brad could snatch her on Halloween night when everyone was in costume. If he had the right costume on, he could have walked up to his sister and she wouldn't have known who he was. He could walk around in the open with no one recognizing him. I wonder if they looked for a costume at the house."

"If he had one, he probably hid it with Rachel's body."

"Yeah, that would make sense. He'd know where all the abandoned

buildings were, and cops know how to break and enter. He probably stashed the body in an empty building. But why not just take it—take her—out in the country and leave her in the woods right then? It wasn't more than a ten-minute drive to get out of town then. He could have done it while he was supposed to be driving around the neighborhood looking for her. Why would he wait and then fix it so the body would be found? It doesn't make any sense."

"Maybe Hatcher didn't even do it. Maybe he was shot by someone who doesn't have anything at all to do with Rachel. Maybe he ticked off one of his tenants or something like that. Or some guy he arrested finally got out of jail and decided to get even. Maybe his wife killed him, like Ryan said."

"Anything's possible, but the timing makes me think it has something to do with Rachel."

"So, do you have some big plan for me? You're not going to let me stay home tomorrow, are you?" I glanced over and caught him smiling.

"You need to talk to Tony Fenton and Holly Wood."

"Jonathan'll kill me if I leave the house."

Charlie shrugged. Nobody was going to kill him. Not that Jonathan really would, of course, but he sure would be mad.

Jonathan had parked in front of the house and was walking out to the mailbox on the street when I opened the garage door with the remote control and drove the Porsche in.

I felt like I'd been away from home for days. Jonathan put my mail down on the chest in the entry, on top of a whole week's worth that I hadn't looked at yet. I never get any interesting mail. All my bills and bank statements go right to my financial manager. I knew there were reports from him and from my stockbroker in the stack of mail, more of the totally incomprehensible reports they're always sending. They could be embezzling all my money and I'd never know. The rest of my mail is magazines and mail order catalogs and ads.

"I'm sleepy," Jonathan said. "I'm not used to getting up so early. You want to take a nap with me?"

"You mean take a nap or"—I tried to waggle my eyebrows, but I'm not very good at it—"'take a *nap*?"

He yawned.

"Go take a nap, Jonathan."

"You could wake me up in a couple hours," he said, waggling his brows just like that Marx Brothers guy. "What are you going to do?"

"I don't know. I need to study a little, things like that."

"Okay. Don't leave." Before heading upstairs, he kissed both my eyebrows—pity-kisses for my lack of waggling ability.

I went into the casual living room and plopped down on the sofa. *"Now what?"* I said to Charlie.

"See if you can get a phone number for Holly Wood."

I picked up the cordless phone from the end table and called Information but there was no phone listed in her name and I didn't know her husband's name. I asked for a listing for Tony or Anthony Fenton. There was an Anthony Fenton with an unpublished number. *"What am I going to ask them anyway? They were only four years old. They won't remember anything important."*

"Maybe they remember something that they don't know is important."

"Are you going to make me track down Sandy Fenton and Billy Offenbach, too? They were only three. I don't remember anything from when I was three."

"Probably not. Who'd you invite to the Halloween party?"

"Some San Jose cops and my neighbors. I went to a dinner party at the Altmans' last month and met a lot of people who live up here. Jonathan

went with me and he said I should invite them all over for dinner, to reciprocate, you know, but I thought a Halloween party wouldn't be so scary. You don't have to worry so much about what fork to use. You remember Mrs. Altman?"

Charlie nodded. We got one of our best clues from Mrs. Altman in April. She owned my house a long time ago and lives a mile or so down the road now.

"She thought it would be fun. She said there hasn't been a big Halloween party in the neighborhood in years."

"Halloween's the day after tomorrow. Don't you have to do something to get ready for it?"

"I'm rich, Charlie. A caterer is bringing the food and the booze and the bartender, and a place called Party Hearty is coming over Halloween morning to decorate the house. They even sent the invitations. And they've hired a band and some guy to take care of parking the cars. All I have to do is pay for it."

"What's your costume?"

"A spider." I remembered my dream, and it made me feel cold, thinking about being caught in a web, trapped, stuck tight in Charlie's web.

"Did you have to come back because of them being cops?"

"I don't know. I think my death knocked things out of kilter. If I hadn't died, maybe I would have been there, maybe I would have solved it. Maybe her killer would have been caught then."

"So everybody doesn't come back. I mean, most dead people don't turn into ghosts, right?"

He smiled, saying, *"It would be a pretty crowded world if they did."*

And it would be a world full of people doing weird things, like me. The world's crazy enough without everyone running around doing what ghosts tell them to do. If Charlie was right, then this really was all his fault. If he hadn't done the things he did that got him killed, he'd have been around to solve Rachel's murder in 1973. And I wouldn't have to be doing it now. Just my luck, to be the one who gets stuck with a ghost.

I fixed us something to eat—soup and a sandwich for me, ghost versions for him—and I watched television for a while, then I told Charlie to go away and stay away until morning. I went upstairs to wake Jonathan up so we could take a nap. Waggle, waggle.

CHAPTER TWENTY-THREE

Jonathan left at seven in the morning, off for another day in court, and not at all happy about it. As soon as he was gone, Charlie told me to call Oak Valley High and see if I could talk to Tony Fenton, the teacher who had been one of the trick-or-treaters. I left a message with the school secretary and Mr. Fenton called back in a few minutes. His planning period was at ten-thirty but he had a short meeting scheduled then. He could meet with me at about eleven, but we'd only have fifteen or twenty minutes before his next class. I said that was fine. Fifteen minutes was more time than I really wanted to spend with a teacher.

After I hung up, I said to Charlie, "You know Jonathan's going to call me every time there's a break, just to be sure I'm here. He'll be really mad if I don't stay home."

"He'll get over it."

Sympathy is not Charlie's strong suit. I spent thirty minutes on the exercise equipment in the rec room in the basement, then I told Charlie to get lost while I showered and dressed. I had to go to class in the afternoon and wasn't sure if I would be able to come home and change beforehand—who knew what Charlie would make me do—so I dressed in jeans, but with a pale green silk shirt instead of one of my old T-shirts.

Before we left I set the phone so it would forward calls to

my cell phone, but I didn't think that would fool Jonathan. You can hear the ring change when the line's being call-forwarded.

Mr. Fenton was all ears and freckles and Adam's apple and knobby wrists; he made me think of Ichabod Crane, although I don't remember Ichabod having red hair. He met me in the office and when we got to his room, he grabbed a student desk from the front of a row and swung it around so it was angled toward the desk behind it, then he carried a chair from behind his teacher's desk and placed it facing the two student desks, so the three seats formed a circle. Three places to sit. Me, him, and . . . Charlie? I looked at my ghost, who shrugged. Tony motioned to one of the desks and I slid in it, saying, "Thank you, Mr. Fenton." He told me to call him Tony.

He had to sort of fold himself up to fit in the desk and I think his knees must have been pressed against the underside of the desktop. He placed a stack of papers in front of him, a red ink pen beside it. The top paper was covered with tiny, scribbly handwriting.

"I was a pumpkin," he said. "My mother made the costume. It was stuffed with newspaper and made a crinkly sound when I moved. That's what I remember most."

Charlie sat down in the chair, sliding it back a little and stretching out his legs. The real chair didn't move, just his ghost chair, so Charlie and the real chair were sort of overlapping. *"Don't do that,"* I said in my mind.

Charlie said, *"Sorry,"* and slid his chair forward until the two chairs became one. He stretched out his legs again. His feet were out of sight, hidden by my desktop. They were probably all mixed up with my own feet but it was all right as long as I didn't have to see them.

"What were the other kids, do you remember?" I asked Tony.

"Ryan was a skelton. He had one of those costumes you buy at the store, like one-piece black pajamas with a white skeleton painted on the front, and a skull mask. My sister was a ballerina. Holly was a clown and Billy was a cowboy. I don't think I really remember that. My mother has a picture of us."

"And Rachel was a ghost."

"Yeah . . . but she isn't in the picture."

"Why not?"

"I don't remember. She must have been somewhere else when it was taken. She was a ghost . . ." He rubbed the back of one bony hand with the back of the other, a faraway look in his eyes. He looked back at me suddenly, seeming almost startled. "It's hard to know what's a memory and what I know from pictures and from hearing about it when I was older. So what's the deal here? You're offering a reward, you said."

"Yes, I am, and I just got curious about the case and decided I'd try to find out as much as I can."

"I don't remember much. I was only four. I called my mother, she's the one you need to talk to. She'll be here in a minute. Well, here she is now," he said, as the door opened.

That explained the third seat; Tony wasn't seeing a ghost after all. As Tony's mother closed the door behind her and crossed the room, I said, *"You get up,"* to Charlie. *"I don't want to have to look at the two of you in the same seat, all overlapping and everything. I'll throw up."*

Charlie got up and stood behind Tony, whose mother looked like what I think of when I hear the word "grandmother," although neither of my grandmothers looks anything like that. She was gray-haired and short and plump and soft-looking— too round to fit in a student desk. Her lap would have been the perfect place for a nap, if you were three years old. I could almost smell oatmeal cookies, fresh from the oven. After putting a big purse on the floor by the desk, she sat down, tugging her navy dress over her knees with one hand while she held a maroon photo album in the other. A pair of glasses hung from a cord around her neck.

"Mom, this is . . . Lizbet? Is that right?"

"Yes, Lizbet Lange. It's nice to meet you, Mrs. Fenton."

"Just call me Alicia. Nice to meet you, too."

Tony had picked up his red pen and now he slashed through a word on the top paper. He drew a line from it to the margin, where he wrote something. My stomach knotted just watching him.

"Tony said you want to hear about the kidnapping. Terrible thing, just terrible. Every mother's worst nightmare. I don't know how Brenda survived it. Not that she did very well. She was never the same afterward, not that she was wrapped too tight before that. She was always so nervous, worrying herself sick over those kids."

"Someone told me she was really nervous when Rebecca was a baby—" I caught myself before I mentioned the other baby because I wasn't sure Alicia knew about that.

"Well, who could blame her? She had another one; you know that, I guess. The poor baby died in her sleep. Sudden Infant Death Syndrome."

I nodded, watching Tony X through an entire half page of some poor kid's essay.

"Who'd you talk to?" Alicia asked. "Lucinda?" When I nodded, she said, "She's a bitch."

"Mother," Tony said, without looking up from the paper he was grading.

She grinned at her son's bent head. "Not in the hallowed

halls, right? Don't make me laugh. These kids today can outcuss a drunken sailor. Lucinda *is* a bitch. Brenda was her best friend and she just dropped her like a hot potato after Rachel died. That poor woman needed her friends then more than ever and Lucinda just turned her back on her. There was some talk . . . well, that's neither here nor there."

"She told me the other parents were mad, too. Because of Brenda taking the children to the apartments."

"Well, I don't guess they were thrilled to find that out—those apartments could get pretty rowdy—but if she'd made it safely home with all the kids, I don't think anyone would have cared that much. I don't recall that anyone was mad at her. Not that any of them had much to do with her afterward, but . . . that was mostly because of Brenda herself. She . . . I don't want to say she went crazy. It wasn't like she was stark raving mad, but she was never the same, that's for sure. It was hard to be around her, hard to see her suffering so much. She just never stopped mourning for Rachel. Not that it would be easy to get over losing a child, especially that way."

"So you were still friends with her afterward?"

"Well, we were never close friends really, more like close acquaintances. She was . . . she wasn't a sociable person, even before the kidnapping. She didn't like having company or visiting other folks. She kept to herself most of the time. After Rachel died, she got worse; she was like a hermit, hardly left the house at all. She even home-schooled Ryan for a couple years. Not too many people were doing that back then but she couldn't stand to let him out of her sight. Our husbands worked together, that's the only reason I ever knew her at all."

Oh, shit. *Another* cop. She would tell him she talked to me, and he'd tell Sterling. "Was your husband involved in the investigation?"

"I guess everyone in the department was in one way or another. Oak Valley was a small town then."

Tony slashed through some words, then wrote furiously. "The English language is being murdered before my very eyes," he said.

"I made Rachel's costume."

"You did?"

"Indeed I did. Not that I didn't have plenty of other things I needed to do that afternoon, plus I was about nine and a half months pregnant and not feeling too good, but Brenda called and asked for help and I dropped everything and stitched up that ghost costume for her. I always felt a little spooked about it, her being killed in the costume I made."

Tony muttered something as his pen bled red across a paper.

"Brenda did some knitting, made really nice sweaters," Alicia said, "but she didn't even own a sewing machine. I made my kids' clothes when they were little. I made Tony the sweetest little outfits. He was such a cutie, with that red hair and those big brown eyes and all those freckles. Just a doll. Sure turned into a cranky old sourpuss, didn't he?"

"*Mother*."

"Anyway, Brenda called me up, all in a tizzy—not that that was unusual for her—and said Rachel couldn't wear the witch costume she'd bought her, it was too small, or too big, I don't really remember. I don't know why she didn't have the girl try it on earlier. You never can trust the sizes on store-bought clothes, you know, especially cheap things. It only took me a few minutes to do the sewing. Brenda had already cut the sheet to fit and marked the eyeholes so all I had to do was cut out the eyes and stitch around them and run a machine hem around the bottom and around the slits in the sides for her hands to go through. Easy as pie."

"This was on Halloween afternoon?"

"Indeed it was. At the last minute, I told you. I gave it to her when I took Tony and Sandy over there. I never did get a chance to see Rachel in it, she was dawdling so about getting ready. She wanted to be a witch and I guess she pitched a fit when the costume didn't fit. Brenda went upstairs to try to hurry her along but I think the girl was sulking. I have a picture of the other kids."

She put her glasses on and opened the photo album, leafing quickly through the pages, then handing the book to me when she found the right one. Five of the six pictures on the page were of Tony and Sandy in their costumes, posing in front of cream-colored draperies. The sixth picture was taken in someone's living room—the Wrights', I assumed. Five kids in costumes: Tony the pumpkin, Sandy the ballerina, Holly the clown, Billy the cowboy, and Ryan the skeleton.

"I never gave a copy to Brenda," Alicia said. "It just seemed too . . ."

"Prophetic," Tony said.

"That's the word. All the kids except Rachel. See what Ryan's doing?"

I saw but I didn't understand. The four younger children were in a row, cute as anything in their brightly colored costumes; Ryan was standing behind them in his skeleton costume, his face covered by a grinning skull mask. He was holding his right arm straight out to the side, his hand bent at the wrist, the fingers curved inward a little.

"Rachel wasn't there, you see. She was still upstairs, pouting about her costume. I wasn't feeling good and I was in a hurry to get back home, so Brenda said to just take the picture without her, so I got the kids lined up and when I was ready to snap the picture, Ryan said something like 'Look, Rachel's here, she's a ghost, she's invisible,' and he put his arm out like that, like he had his arm around her. It was kind of funny at the time, but afterward it just spooked me, because Rachel died a little while later. It was like an omen, Rachel being a ghost, being invisible. No, I never gave Brenda a copy. I thought it would make her sad to see it."

It gave me the chills. Tony had stopped reading the essays and was staring at his mother. He hunched his shoulders and I thought I saw him shudder; he must have felt the way I did.

I closed the album cover and traced my finger over the raised letters of the word MEMORIES that was on the front. I was trying to add up the cops. Larry Wright and Brad Hatcher. Lucinda Todd's husband, Luther. Tony and Sandy's father. Holly Brown's father. The newspaper articles hadn't mentioned that their fathers were all cops. I suppose it was to protect them from all the publicity. Or maybe they thought it was bad publicity for the police department. "Was Billy Offenbach's father a cop, too?"

"Dispatcher. He was in a wheelchair, lost both legs in a motorcycle accident when he was a teenager. They moved away years ago."

"There sure were a lot of cops in that neighborhood."

She laughed. "Sure were. We called it Cop City. It was the first new housing development in Oak Valley in years. There was a regular housing shortage before that. There must have been, oh, easily a dozen of us altogether in the neighborhood. A few years later—middle 'seventies—real estate prices went through the roof. We sold our house eight years after we bought it and got twice what we paid for it. Best investment we ever made."

"Paid for my college," Tony said, as if he knew that was the next thing his mother would say.

"Paid for Tony's college, that's right. Both his sisters', too. So what do you do, dear?"

"I'm not working right now." I glanced at Charlie, knowing I'd made it sound like I had a glamorous profession that I just might return to any minute. I didn't feel like telling them that I'd never been anything but a waitress. "I inherited some money. A lot of money, actually."

"Well, that's nice. Everyone should have a rich relative. We're going to spend Tony's inheritance." She reached over and patted his hand. "Isn't that right, hon?" Tony grimaced and scratched out a few words. His mother said, "We sold our house in April and moved into an apartment. We just bought us a great big motorhome. Doug's retiring at the end of the year and we're going to travel all over the country."

I was telling her that sounded like fun when my purse rang. I dug the cell phone out of it. It was Jonathan, of course. "Are you home?" he asked, sounding suspicious. "The phone rang funny."

"I'm at the high school, talking to the teacher."

With absolutely perfect timing, the passing bell rang, so loud it made my hand jerk and I almost dropped the phone. Jonathan couldn't help but hear it over the phone. "There's the bell," I said. "He has a class now so I need to hurry up." The building practically shook with the sound of a thousand teenagers being set loose.

"You were supposed to stay home."

"I needed to talk to the teacher."

"All right, but go home, okay? And stay there. We're on a lunch break. I'll call you if we get another break this afternoon. I still haven't been called. What a waste of time. Hold on." I heard him say "Thanks" to someone else, the phone tipped away from his face so his voice was faint, then he said to me, "My food's here. I'll call you later. You're going home now, right?"

"My class is today, so I won't be home if you call then. See you later." I disconnected quickly and turned the phone off, smiling to myself because I made it through the entire conversation without lying.

It sounded like there was a riot going on in the hall. The door banged opened and five or six kids came in, all talking at once. Tony got up and slid his desk back into position. I thanked him for letting me come, then his mother and I left together, squeezing past the kids coming into the room. Getting through the hall was like playing some crazy game of dodge ball, but it was teenagers you were dodging, not balls. We finally made it out the front door.

At the top of the steps leading to the sidewalk, Alicia turned to me, saying, "Tony never liked to talk about the kidnapping, not even after he was grown. He had nightmares for months after it happened. He'd wake up in the night and come get in bed with us. He kept saying that Rachel was a ghost, over and over. I think that costume made it worse for him. He got it all mixed up in his head. He knew a ghost was supposed to be a dead person, and Rachel was a ghost, so she was dead. Like the costume had something to do with it, you know. He was so little he couldn't say all his sounds right. I can still hear him: 'Waychel's im*bis*ible, Mama. I can't *see* her.' Made my blood run cold, hearing him say that, indeed it did. Here's Doug. You never can find a parking place around the school so he took an early lunch break and drove me over."

She was looking at a man who was getting out of a car parked in the No Parking zone. It wasn't a police car, but he was dressed in a blue Oak Valley Police Department uniform. The brass on his hat meant he was a lieutenant. He smiled at his wife as he walked up the stairs to join us, looking so happy to see her that they might have been married yesterday instead of long ago.

"This is Lizbet Lange, Doug. Lizbet, my husband, Doug Fenton."

He looked ten years younger than his wife, although they were probably about the same age. He was either completely bald or he shaved his head, but he was one of those men who were made to be bald, like Yul Brynner and Michael Jordan. His eyes were blue, his teeth very white against his tan skin, his posture perfect. He could have played the good cop in a movie, and everyone would have been stunned if he turned out to be the bad guy. Like a ghost I know, I thought, glancing at Charlie, who must have heard what I was thinking because he shrugged, looking sheepish.

"Nice to meet you, Lizbet," Lieutenant Fenton said. "John Sterling and I were talking about you just this morning." He was grinning, making me wonder just exactly what Sterling had said. "If there's one thing I'd like to see happen before I retire, it's the Rachel Wright case being solved. I don't know if your reward will do any good but it's sure nice of you to offer it."

"I hope it helps." My stomach was cramping; he'd probably tell Sterling he talked to me as soon as he got back to work. Maybe he'd already told Sterling his wife and his son were meeting with me. Sterling could already be seething.

"It was hard on everyone in the department, having a cop's kid murdered and never catching the guy who did it. I don't know how many times I've read the reports over the years, hoping I'd see something that everyone missed. Never did though."

Charlie said, *"Ask him about Hatcher."*

"Ask him what?"

"If he thinks there's a connection."

I asked. Doug said, "It's a pretty big coincidence, if there isn't. It's hard to imagine what it is though, after all these years."

"What if Brad Hatcher was the killer?"

"That's Sterling's theory, but I can't really buy it. There just wasn't enough time for him to do it, if you ask me, and he was taking a hell of a risk if he had the body in his car, and I don't see how he thought he'd have time to take it anyplace before Brenda reported the girl missing."

"Nobody searched his car. They let him leave in it."

"Yeah, but what if they hadn't? If he did it, he was just lucky it was Sterling who responded, instead of me. I'd have searched the cars and the house first thing, just as a matter of routine, so I could say I followed procedure if the girl didn't turn up safe." Smiling at his wife, he said, "You ready to go, honey? I need to get back to work. Nice meeting you," he said to me again as they walked off, holding hands.

On the walk to the car, which was a couple blocks away, I asked Charlie if he really thought Brad Hatcher killed his niece.

"I don't know. Fenton's right, it was pretty risky. But maybe he thought he'd have more time; maybe he didn't think Brenda would panic. He could have assumed she'd come home first and he could leave then, pretending he was going out looking for Rachel. He probably thought she'd come home and tell her husband as soon as she missed the girl, instead of calling the

cops right away. That still bothers me, that she didn't go home to see if Rachel was there."

"She just wasn't thinking right. Everyone says she panicked, and she was a really nervous person anyway."

"I could believe that if her husband wasn't a cop. If Jonathan had ever disappeared, Amanda would have called me first, unless she knew for sure she couldn't get hold of me in a hurry. She knew I'd know how to set the machinery in motion. Besides, she'd want me to know right away, not after some other cop showed up to take a report."

"But, Charlie, Brenda couldn't have done it—what would she have done with the body?—and I can't see her covering for her brother, not if he killed her child. I mean, I know he was her brother and I guess brothers and sisters are pretty close, but still—not if he killed her child."

"What if Larry Wright did it?"

"Do you mean would she lie to protect her husband? I don't know. I don't think he did it. He's too . . . normal."

"That leaves Brad Hatcher."

"Or a total stranger."

"I don't think I'd be here if it was a total stranger. It's someone who's still around, still in a position to cause trouble."

"If Brad Hatcher did it, he can't hurt anyone else since he's dead, so it should be over, shouldn't it?"

"I'd be gone if it was over."

I turned my head, looking away from him, not wanting him to see the tears in my eyes. I didn't want him to leave, I didn't want to miss him, not even for the few days it would take for me to forget all about him.

CHAPTER TWENTY-FOUR

Our next stop was the bank where Holly Wood worked. She was there and she was easy to find because HOLLY WOOD was on a name plate on her desk, which was out in the middle of the lobby near three other desks with no one sitting at them. She wasn't doing anything so I sat down and she smiled and asked how she could help me.

"I'm putting up a reward for information about Rachel Wright's murder and I'm trying to find out as much as I can about the case. I understand you were one of the trick-or-treaters with her."

Holly Wood was wearing a brown, dark green, and cream top that Jill would have described as an "ethnic print," a big splashy abstract pattern that looked vaguely jungly. She was slender, with light brown freckled skin. I suspected she was tall, but couldn't tell since she was sitting down. She had a long nose with a pair of round rimless glasses perched on it, a long chin, and long reddish brown hair in tight waves, like it had been braided then brushed out. Her eyes were light yellowish-brown, almost golden, with lashes I would have killed for. Her eyebrows shot up when I told her why I was there. She looked around, even turning to look behind her, like she was checking to see if anyone could hear us.

She leaned toward me across the desk, speaking low: "Are you from the police?"

Why would she think I was from the police? Was she expecting them? I told her no and explained again about the money.

"A reward?" she said. She started tapping a pen against the desk—tappity-tappity-tappity—and after every sentence she paused for second and bit her lower lip. "Well, that's a good idea, I guess." Bite. "But it was so long ago." Bite. "I don't really remember much about it." Bite. "I was only four." Bite. She was so nervous she was making me nervous. I felt myself bite my own lip.

"Did Brenda Wright leave?"

She blinked rapidly, blinking back tears, her eyes wide. "They sent you, didn't they? The police?" Bite.

Before I could say no, Charlie said, *"Let her think they did."* So I didn't say anything.

Tappity-tappity-tappity. "I can't talk about it here, not at work. Can I meet you later? I don't know why . . . I hadn't thought about it in . . . in just about forever." Bite.

"When do you get off work?"

"Not 'til six, but my lunch break is at twelve-thirty." She stood up and she really was tall, probably almost six feet, and she was even taller than that because she was wearing shoes with thick platform soles. They had straps that wrapped around her legs and disappeared under the hem of a long brown skirt. She walked around the desk, so I stood up, too. She said, "I just can't . . . I can't talk about it here. There's a bar called Jacob's, right down the street. Um, you're over twenty-one, right?"

"Yes." But they would card me anyway; they always do. "I know where Jacob's is."

"Okay, I'll meet you there at twelve-thirty, a few minutes

after." She touched my arm for just a second, a signal for me to come with her, then she started walking toward the door, staying close to my side, whispering, leaning down a bit so I'd be sure to hear her. "The billboard . . . I saw the billboard. The day before yesterday. I hadn't seen it before. But we drove by and . . . and I started crying, I just started crying. I couldn't stop." Bite. "My husband . . . it scared him. He couldn't understand why I was so upset. I couldn't come to work yesterday, I was just too upset. It was the first time I've thought about it in years." Bite. "Years and years. I kept thinking about it, worrying about it. I thought I had to do something." Bite. "My husband's going with me. To the police. He made an appointment. Tomorrow morning. Our lawyer's going with us. My husband said we should have a lawyer with us, just . . . just to be on the safe side." Bite. "I was so young. It was so long ago. But I have to tell someone." Bite.

As the automatic doors opened, Holly Wood stopped and stood straight and smiled perkily, so her co-workers would think I was a customer, I guess. I told her I'd see her at Jacob's.

"Boy, was she nervous," I said to Charlie when we were outside.

He grinned, looking happy. Cops get high on good leads. *"Nervous as hell,"* he said. *"What time is it?"*

I thought a ghost should know, but Charlie doesn't wear a watch, and who knows what time zone he's in anyway. *"Eleven-forty. I need to go to the library and get a book. I have some homework. We have to read a classic and find twenty-five words in it we don't know and look them up in the dictionary."*

"You have a whole room of classics at home."

"Yeah, but they're all old stuff. Shakespeare and Charles Dickens

and . . . people like that. He said we can pick a modern classic, whatever that means. He gave us a list of authors. I have it in my purse."

At the library, I dug around in my purse and found the paper and unfolded it. Charlie took it—a ghost copy that floated off the real paper—and ran his finger down the list. *"Pick one by James Joyce. It'll be loaded with words you don't know."*

I wondered if I should be insulted. I checked out a copy of *The Dubliners* because it was the first one I saw on the shelf, and then we found a parking place near Jacob's. Since I had time to kill, I started reading the book, just skimming it really, looking for unfamiliar words. This was going to be easy. I found *gnomen* and *simony* and *maleficent* on the first page. I couldn't even figure out *gnomen* and *simony* from the context. The GED teacher is big on context. Think about the context, he's always saying, and you can often figure out the meaning. I guess he's right but I don't know why he has to say it over and over again. I jotted the words on the back of a parking ticket I'd taken from the dashbox. I knew *maleficent* meant "evil" or something like that, but I figured the teacher couldn't prove I already knew it. By twelve-thirty I'd written down *nipper, stirabout*—which I wondered if I'd even find in the dictionary since it seemed to be some kind of Irish food—*simoniac, inefficacious, catacombs, venial,* and *elucidating,* and five or six other words and I was only on page 20. That guy knew a lot of words.

Holly wasn't at Jacob's when we got there so we went on in and found a booth near the back. The bar was quiet and dark, furnished to look like a British pub, with dart boards and those horns they blow at fox hunts. *"Are you going to order something?"* Charlie asked. *"A shot of tequila sounds good."*

"You aren't going to get drunk on me, are you?" Holly and the waitress arrived just then. I smiled at Holly and said, "A Bloody

Mary, please," to the waitress. I already had my wallet out and held it so she could see my driver's license.

"That sounds good," Holly said, sliding into the booth. "Same for me."

I wondered if she always drank her lunch. I had automatically moved all the way over in the booth to make room for Charlie to sit beside me, and Holly slid over on her bench so she was facing me. She didn't seem to find it odd that I was sitting over against the wall, my right shoulder actually touching it because I didn't want to touch Charlie. I never had; just the thought of it gave me the creeps. I was pretty sure I wouldn't feel him at all, but what if I did?

Holly chattered about the weather and the traffic until the waitress arrived with the drinks. As soon as she left, Charlie slid a ghost glass out of my glass and took a long drink. I picked up the real glass and took a tiny sip and set it down again. It was too cold, and bitter. I wished I'd ordered a soft drink instead.

"I don't know why I'm doing this," Holly said. "I don't know if I should be talking to you."

"The police know I'm talking to people. I spoke to the chief of police about it, Chief Sterling."

"Did you? Oh, well, then . . . God, I feel so . . . I don't know what. I haven't talked about it, haven't even thought about it for years and years. But . . . the billboard. It really shook me up. Brought it all back, you know. Oh, god. I kept it secret for so long, and now . . . now I feel *guilty*. I don't know why I never told anyone. No, I do know why: because I didn't think it was real." She was crying, not making any sound, just tears running down her cheeks. She flicked them away with her index fingers, almost like she didn't realize she was crying, she just knew something was tickling her face.

"You didn't think what was real? Rachel being kidnapped?"

"No, although . . . I don't think I really understood what happened to her until I was a lot older. I don't think my parents told me her body was found. I guess I sort of knew what kidnapping was, but they didn't talk about it around me. I was too young. I really didn't understand it." She took a tiny sip of her drink, and shivered so hard that I could see her do it. She wrapped her arms around herself, briskly rubbing her upper arms with her hands. "Brrr. Is it cold in here to you?"

The bar seemed warm to me, but she didn't wait for an answer.

"No one has asked me about the kidnapping in years. I don't know how much I really remember. A lot of it . . . I think I just remember my parents talking about it later. They never let me leave the house on Halloween again, not ever." She took another little sip of her drink, not shivering this time but staring into the glass afterward, moving it slightly so the ice tinkled like a miniature wind chime. "I remember being scared, not after she disappeared but before that. All the costumes, they scared me. I don't think I understood what Halloween was all about, but my mother dressed me up in a little clown costume she made and sent me out with Rachel's mother.

"I wanted to hold her hand and she kept telling me to be a big girl. I remember thinking that she didn't want to hold my hand"—Holly looked up from her glass, looking me right in the eye—"because I'm black. I knew about that already, about how some people feel, even back then, when I was only four. We were the only black family in the neighborhood then. But I did hold her hand for a while, I remember that, and I felt better. Safer, you know. It was so scary—being outside in the dark, and all the costumes, and some of the houses had tape recordings playing scary sounds, howls and shrieks and ghost sounds. Halloween . . . I think it should be abolished. People think it's fun for little kids, but it's just scary. I don't have any children yet, but I think if I do I'll skip the whole Halloween thing."

She gazed off behind me for a moment then said, "I remember Rachel's mother calling her. I remember her crying. I remember people shouting and running and cop cars with their lights flashing, but I don't think I knew what was going on. I remember my parents showing up and my dad picking me up and carrying me home. I remember his hands were shaking and he was holding me too tight and he kept saying 'It's okay, everything's going to be okay' over and over again, but I didn't understand what was wrong. I'm not sure I even understood that Rachel had been kidnapped, I just knew all the grownups were upset and that scared me."

"But you remember something, right? What are you going to the police for?"

She stared at me for a moment, wide-eyed, then she shrugged one thin shoulder, and leaned across the table toward me, and whispered, "Rachel was a ghost."

I glanced at the ghost beside me. "A ghost?"

"Her costume," Charlie said, *"she was wearing a ghost costume."*

"Oh, yeah. I mean, I know. Tony Fenton's mom made her a ghost costume."

Holly smiled, a wobbly smile that made her chin pucker. "She was a ghost. She was . . . a *ghost.*" And then she started crying, and she slid out of the booth, saying, "I'm sorry, I just can't do this," and she was gone, running toward the door, her tall shoes smacking hard on the tile, the other people in the bar all turning to watch her go, then turning to look at me, curiosity on their faces. The door closed behind her, the bar seeming even darker after the brief burst of bright sunshine. I looked at Charlie, feeling stunned.

He said, *"That was interesting."*

I thought it was sad, and mean of me to make her think about something that had happened so long ago, something that was so traumatic she couldn't talk about it, even after all these years.

Chapter Twenty-five

Even Charlie couldn't think of anything else to do, so we went home. I went into the library and worked on my word list, finding the twenty-fifth word—*scudding*—on page 42 and typing them all on the computer, along with definitions from the dictionary. *Stirabout* is a kind of porridge.

When I was finished, I logged on to the Internet, thinking Charlie would find it interesting, but he doesn't really seem surprised by all the things that didn't exist when he was alive, like home computers, cordless phones and cell phones, microwaves, CDs, cable TV. It's like he already knows all about them. They didn't have those things in 1973, either. There really wasn't much of anything new that year.

Biggest technological advance in 'seventy-three was the push-through tab on beer cans, Duke says, popping the top on a can after dropping his joint in an empty one.

That was a big improvement, Lady says. *At least I didn't step on them in my bare feet. Before that you pulled the tabs right off,* she says to me. *And you dropped them on the floor.* She's looking at Duke, who surprises me by smiling at her.

They launched Skylab, he says.

Yeah, they were sending men to outer space, and down here we were standing in line to buy gas, and paying a fortune for it.

Arab oil embargo, Duke says. *Drove the cost of gas sky high.*
What's that mean, Duke? Embargo?

But he's busy rolling another joint and Lady says she has to
wash the dishes, so I never find out.

Since I had the computer on anyway, I read Jonathan's e-
mail. Most of the messages were jokes cops had sent him and
he'd already told them to me, except the ones that were sexist. I
thought about going to the newsgroups to see if I could figure
out what he found so fascinating about them, but I thought I
wouldn't understand anyway. I mean, he's around cops all the
time at work so why would he want to come home and read a
bunch of newsgroup posts from cops he doesn't even know? It
would be like me e-mailing a salesclerk at Sears to talk about
clothes, when I could just go down to Jill's Jeans 'n Things or
Madame and Eve's Boutique and try some on. I logged off.

"Let's talk about the case," Charlie said.

I spun the chair around to face him. "Like what?"

"The things that don't make sense."

"You mean like Brenda not going home to look for Rachel?"

"That's one of them."

"What else? . . . You know what doesn't make sense? If it
was her uncle, or her parents, why did they hide the body for
three days? That's just sickening, stashing a dead body somewhere and then *moving* it three days later—god, that's yucky. I
mean, bodies . . . rot, right?"

"And then her body was left where it would be sure to be found.
Why?"

"He—or she or whoever—wanted the body to be found."

"Why?"

"I don't know."

"What if the body was never found?"

"No one would ever know for sure that she was dead. Except whoever killed her."

"And?"

"The police would keep searching for her."

"And?"

"Well, they wouldn't have a funeral unless they were pretty sure she was dead. Sometimes people have memorial services even if a body's never found, but that's when they know for sure the person is dead but they just can't find the body. Like it was thrown in the ocean or the killer confessed but couldn't remember where he buried it."

"And if there was no funeral, if her body was never found?"

What if Duke and Lady had just disappeared? What if one day they were just gone, nothing left but their trailer and their clothes and cars and photo albums and their record collection, all their things left as if they were coming back to them, but they never came back.

What if I had never found out what happened to them? What if I had to spend the rest of my life wondering if they were dead or alive, never knowing for sure, never knowing if the next time the phone rang, the next time there was a knock on the door, it would be them; never knowing, always hoping.

"It would be harder on the parents to never know. People are always talking about needing closure. There's no closure if you never know for sure, and that's even harder than losing someone."

If you know someone's dead, you mourn and then you go on. But if they never knew whether Rachel was dead or alive, they'd spend the rest of their lives waiting for her to be found, hoping she'd be found. They'd see a little girl—then later a teenager and, even later, a young woman—someone who looked a little like her, and for just a heartbeat they'd think they'd found her at last. Each time would make it worse, the constant hoping, the constant disappointment, wondering every time they heard about a long-buried body being found if it was Rachel, hoping it wasn't, but also hoping it was so it would be over, because if they never knew for sure, it would never end, it would never, ever end.

"It had to be one of her parents then. Isn't that right? One of them killed her, and didn't want the other one to never have closure. It has to be Larry. Brenda couldn't have done it. She had the little kids with her. She couldn't leave them. But Larry was watching the baby. Wait, Charlie: That doesn't make sense either. Why would one of her parents move the body later? Why not make sure she was found right away? Moving the body had to be just awful."

Charlie was smiling. *"I think that's the right question: Why wait three days?"*

"Because . . . because there would be an autopsy. There always is when someone's murdered."

"Bingo."

I spun the chair back and stared at the computer screen, where tiny stars were rushing toward me from a black void. The stars zoomed off the edge of the screen, an endless stream of new stars appearing at the center then whooshing out of sight. Sterling had the autopsy report on his desk: Post mortem interval. Post mortem lividity. Degree of putrefaction. Gastric contents. "Oh, Charlie. Oh, Charlie, she *couldn't* be a witch, she had to be a *ghost*. We need to go back to the Wrights' house."

"One of them killed her. It had to be one of them. They wouldn't do it for Hatcher. They'd have turned him in. You need to come up with

a good reason to talk to them again. You don't want to make them suspicious."

I watched the stars flying for a couple minutes. *Devious* isn't my middle name but it should be. When I was a teenager, my whole life was a secret that I kept from Duke and Lady, and they never questioned my cover stories because they were so good. I came up with a plan and when I explained it to Charlie, he smiled his glorious smile. *"Jonathan was right,"* he said. *"Lizbet Lange, Girl Sleuth."*

I checked the yellow pages, then called a store in San Jose called For Keeps. The woman I spoke to had just what I needed. After giving her my credit card number, I called the Oak Valley Taxi Company and arranged to have a package picked up and delivered to my house. Another charge went on my credit card, and a taxi driver somewhere in Oak Valley was dispatched to San Jose. Less than an hour later he rang the doorbell and handed me a bag, then left with a big tip in his pocket and a big smile on his face. Some things are just so easy when it doesn't matter how much it costs.

"We need to go right now, Charlie. If we don't hurry, I'll never make it to my class on time. Do you think I should call first?"

"No, let's just go."

It didn't take long to get to the condo, since I knew right where it was this time. Larry Wright opened the door, looking puzzled.

"Hi," I said. "I have something for your wife."

"What?"

"She'll like it." I pulled a box out of the For Keeps bag: Barbie with dark pigtails, dressed as Dorothy from *The Wizard of Oz*, in a blue gingham dress with a white lace cotton petticoat showing beneath it, and ruby red slippers. Toto was in a basket hanging from her arm. "Someone gave it to me, but I don't collect them and I know Brenda would love to have it. It's a collector's edition. Mint condition, never removed from the box." For Keeps also had a Barbie dressed as Glinda the Good Witch, but I thought that would have been just a little too cruel.

"Well, I—well, it's real nice of you. Come on in. She's upstairs, I think."

"Oh, good, I'd like to see it with the other ones. I can help her find a place to display it."

"Uh, yeah, sure." He called up the stairs: "Brenda? Lizbet Lange's here again. She has something for you."

Brenda said something that I didn't quite hear. "Go on up," Larry said.

She was in Rachel's room, sitting in the white wicker rocker. The Barbies that had been on the chair were now on the floor at her feet. She'd been crying. She'd just buried her brother and tomorrow would be the anniversary of her daughter's death, but even so I couldn't help but wonder if she *ever* stopped.

"I have a present for you," I said. "I don't need it and I thought it should have a good home. Here." I handed her the Barbie box.

She held it in front of her at arm's length. "Oh, it's beautiful. But, really, I can't take it."

"Please. I want you to have it. You're the only person I know who collects them."

"Well . . . if you're sure."

"I'm sure. Where should we put it?"

She stood up, looking around the room. I spotted the pink photo album on the dresser. "Could I look at her album again?" I asked.

She nodded absently, walking to the glass-fronted cabinet.

I opened the album and turned the pages, chatting non-stop, telling Brenda about the class Lady and I had taken, and how I was going to put all my photos in albums like hers, and what a good job she'd done on Rachel's album. When I found the right page, I checked over my shoulder. Brenda had opened the cabinet door and was moving dolls around on the top shelf.

I surreptitiously peeled a photo off the page, then quickly flipped to the next page. *Surreptitious* is one of my vocabulary words, of course. I slid the photo into the side pocket of my purse, not daring to take the time to look at the back of it.

"What do you think?" Brenda asked, making me jump.

I closed the album and turned to face her. "It looks good there, it's perfect."

She smiled, taking another look at her new Barbie doll in its place of honor in the center of the top shelf. She closed the cabinet door, then stepped back to admire the display again.

I felt slimy. Last time Charlie showed up I ended up stealing something, too.

"Get out fast now," Charlie said. *"You don't want her to look at the album while you're here."*

Glancing at my watch, I said, "Oh, good grief. It's later than I thought. I'm taking a class and it starts pretty soon. I'd better be going." I walked to the door while I talked, and I kept rattling on and on about how I hadn't realized how late it was getting as I stepped into the hall. Brenda went downstairs with me, thanking me again for the doll. Larry wasn't in sight. I said goodbye to Brenda, assuring her again that I really didn't want the doll and that I was glad to give it to someone who would appreciate it.

I had to force myself not to run to the car.

CHAPTER TWENTY-SIX

I pulled over to the curb a few blocks away from the condo and took the photo out of my purse, my stomach flopping over when I saw what was written on the back.

"Now what? Sterling's office, right?"

"Right," Charlie said.

Sterling's secretary buzzed him and told him I was there before I could say a word. She even got my name right. After pointing to his door, she turned back to her computer.

I took my usual seat in front of Sterling's desk and didn't wait for him to ask me why I was there. "Do you know about Rachel's Halloween costume?"

"I know you haven't spent much time at home today." He waited to see if I was going to respond to that. When I didn't, he said, "She was wearing it when her body was found. Why?"

"That was a ghost costume. She was going to be a witch, but Brenda called Alicia Fenton and asked if she'd sew up a sheet to make a ghost costume because the witch costume didn't fit. That was Halloween afternoon."

He nodded slowly. "Okay. I don't think I knew that. If someone mentioned it then . . ." He shrugged. "Why is it important?"

I handed him the picture.

"This is Rachel. Where'd you get it?"

"I stole it. Turn it over."

He glanced at the date written on the back: October 31, 1973. Rachel posed for a Halloween picture for the first time when she was two, for the last time when she was ten.

"Well?"

"Well, don't you get it?"

"Get what? Rachel had a witch costume. She put it on for a picture. So?"

"I already told you: Brenda told Alicia Fenton the witch costume didn't fit."

He looked at the picture, at the date, at the picture again. "You also told me Brenda asked Alicia to do her a favor, to sew a costume at the last minute, right?"

"Right."

"So Rachel decided she didn't want to be a witch, and her mother got her another costume. I'm assuming Brenda couldn't make a ghost costume herself for some reason?"

"She didn't sew. She didn't have a machine."

"So she asks a friend to do her a last-minute favor. And she lies and says the costume doesn't fit, instead of telling the truth: her daughter was throwing a temper tantrum and she was giving in to her and getting her what she wanted—a different costume."

"You don't know that."

"No, I'm just speculating. Which I suspect is what you're doing. Why don't you tell me what *your* theory is."

"Name one person who saw Rachel in her ghost costume."

"Her mother, her brother, the other children, probably her uncle, although I don't know that for sure. The people whose houses they went to."

"Not counting the little kids and a bunch of strangers—*strangers*, because she didn't go to her neighbors' houses, she went to the apartments—not counting them, who do you know for *sure* saw her in her ghost costume?"

"Her mother, her brother. Maybe her uncle."

"Anyone else?"

"We tried to find people who saw her, trying to pinpoint the time. People remembered seeing a ghost, more than one—it's an easy costume to make—but remembering whether a particular ghost was with a particular group . . . There were too many kids in costumes, too many people ringing doorbells. You answer the door, there's a bunch of trick-or-treaters, you drop candy in their bags, they're gone."

"If Brenda had taken the kids trick-or-treating at houses where she knew the people, someone would have noticed if Rachel wasn't with her."

"And that's what you think? That Rachel wasn't with her?"

"I think she was already dead."

"Already dead? Because of this?" He held the picture up.

"Because of that. And because her body was hidden for three days. Because by then there was no way you could tell for sure when she died. Because the time of death was determined by the fact that her mother said she ate a tuna sandwich and potato chips for dinner. Because a tuna sandwich is lunch, not dinner. Because—"

He held up both hands, palms out. "Whoa. Wait. Wait a minute. You think Brenda Wright killed her *own daughter*, and then came up with an elaborate scheme to cover it up? You think she hid the body somewhere, pretended Rachel was still alive, and then faked a kidnapping so she could get away with murder? Is that what you think? You think she convinced her own son and four other children to lie about it, and not just to lie about it then, but to never say a word about it for the rest of their *lives*. Is that what you think?"

"Yes."

He shook his head. "She loved her children, loved them almost too much. If she killed one of them she would have been found beside the body, crying, hysterical, out of her mind. You've met her. Do you really think she's a cold-blooded killer capable of pulling off something like that?"

I looked up at Charlie, who was standing beside my chair. *"It is kind of hard to believe, isn't it?"*

"Don't look at me. And remember what Tony Fenton said."

I looked away, trying to keep my face expressionless. *"Rachel was a ghost. Rachel was invisible."* Out loud, I said, "I remember my first trip to Disneyland. We went during Christmas vacation when I was in kindergarten. I had my picture taken with Mickey Mouse and Goofy. I was afraid of them. They were so big. I didn't understand they were just people in costumes. Maybe I would have but Duke and Lady were acting like it was really Mickey and Goofy. If they'd told me they were just people in costumes, I would have understood that, but they wanted me to believe they were real, and I *did* believe it, because Duke and Lady told me so. Brenda told those little kids that Rachel was a ghost, that's why they couldn't see her. She told them Rachel was there but they couldn't see her because she was a ghost and ghosts are invisible. They were just little kids. Billy Offenbach and Tony's sister probably don't remember anything about it, but Tony and Holly were a little older. Maybe it was confusing to them, but they believed her. Kids a lot older than that believe in the tooth fairy and Santa Claus. Children are scared of clowns because they don't understand a clown is just a person with makeup on. They think Big Bird is real. They think there are monsters under the bed."

"But they didn't stay children forever. They grew up."

"They forgot about it. How much do you remember from when you were four?"

Sterling smiled a little. "That was a long time ago."

"But even when you were ten, or twenty, how much did you remember *then* about being four years old?"

"Not much, I guess."

"They wouldn't have wanted to remember it either. It was scary. They would want to forget about it. Could I make a phone call?" He shoved his phone toward me. "I need Lieutenant Fenton's home phone number."

"Why?"

"Because."

He sighed, and spun his Rolodex, then plucked a card out of it and handed to me.

"Is there some way you can listen in?"

"From Rosemary's phone."

He didn't move though, so I said, "You really should hear this."

I started tapping out the numbers. He went into his secretary's office, leaving the connecting door open, standing where he could see me, the phone cord stretched across the room.

Alicia seemed a little surprised to hear from me. "I just have a question," I told her. "Brenda gave you a sheet for the costume. Did she bring it to your house?"

"Um . . . no. She must have sent one of the kids. Let me think . . . Ryan brought it over. That's right. I remember I gave him a cookie, told him he was a good boy for bringing it right over, and I told him to go straight home. He got distracted easily, you know, had some learning problems."

"Ryan," I said. "Thank you. Oh, one more thing: You started

to say something when I saw you today, something about there being some talk about Brenda, but you stopped. What was it? Will you tell me?"

She was silent for a moment, then said, "Well, it's water under a very old bridge, isn't it? so I guess it can't hurt. The talk was that Brenda was having an affair with Lucinda's husband. With Luther Todd. I always thought that was why Lucinda stopped being friends with her. I figured maybe when Brenda was so upset over Rachel, Luther let something slip, let his wife know he was involved with her. Maybe it was just obvious that he was more concerned about her than a man should be about another man's wife. I never knew for sure. It was just gossip."

Phooey. I'd been hoping it was something important. I didn't care who was sleeping with who. Or whom. Or whatever. I assured her I wouldn't mention it to anyone, and told her goodbye.

Sterling stood in the doorway, leaning a shoulder against the doorjamb.

"Ryan was the kind of kid you didn't send on errands if you wanted them done right, isn't that what you told me? But she sent him. *Him*, not Rachel. The costume was for Rachel. It would have made more sense for her to go so Alicia could have her try it on. What hours was Larry Wright working?"

"It's in the report somewhere." He went to his desk, flipping through papers in a file folder. "Nine to six."

"Why'd it take him forty minutes to get home?"

"I remember that. He did go home right after work, but he left again right away. Brenda told him she needed something for the baby, cough syrup or baby aspirin, some kind of medicine, and she gave him a list of a few other things to pick up at the store since he was going anyway. He was gone about half an hour."

"And they were gone when he got home, right?"

"Yeah, Hatcher was there to watch Rebecca, so Brenda went ahead and took the kids out."

"Did anyone ever ask Larry if he saw Rachel while he was home, before he left for the store?"

"I doubt it. Why would we? Rachel went trick-or-treating with her mother. There was no reason for us to doubt that."

"She picked a fight with Lucinda so there wouldn't be anyone with her except the four little kids and Ryan."

"I know they had a fight."

"She did it on purpose. She needed to get rid of Lucinda. She couldn't have an adult with her, or Lucinda's kids. They were too old."

"Not much older than Ryan."

"But Ryan . . . well, he's a little odd, isn't he? Besides, Brenda was his mother, he'd do what she said. He'd keep a secret if she told him to."

Sterling's phone rang. He answered it and talked for a couple minutes. I didn't pay any attention to what he was saying. I was thinking about secrets.

I'm nine years old. It's early morning, still half-dark, long before my alarm is set to go off, but Lady is shaking me awake. *Lizbet, sit up and listen to me. Are you awake?*

What's wrong? I ask, the urgency in her voice scaring me. She's dressed all in white, ready to leave for the cannery, where she and Duke both work the early shift.

Her voice is low, whispery, scary. *You have to stay home from school today. I want you here when the mail comes. You watch for the mailman and you bring the mail in right away, do you hear me?*

I can hear Duke in the driveway, trying to start the car, the starter grinding again and again.

Why, Lady? I'm not sick.

I know that. I need you here, that's why. Watch for the mailman, he comes about ten. Get the mail right away, just as soon as it comes, okay?

Okay, but why—

There'll be a letter addressed to me. You take it and put it in my underwear drawer. Put it down under the clothes. Put the rest of the mail back in the mailbox. I'll bring it in when we come home from work. And don't you say anything to Duke, do you understand? I'm going to tell him you have a stomachache.

What's the letter about? Is it something bad?

Outside, the car finally starts, the engine revving loudly, then Duke honks the horn, three quick taps.

Lady looks over her shoulder at the closed door of my room. *It's nothing. It's just . . . they weren't supposed to mail it, I was going to pick it up, but that stupid woman in the office—It isn't anything important. Just do what I tell you, and, Lizbet: Don't tell Duke.*

The letter doesn't come, and that evening the lines by Lady's mouth seem deeper. I have a stomachache the next day, too, and the letter arrives, along with the phone bill and an ad from J. C. Penney. I study the envelope carefully; it's long and white, smooth, secretive. It's addressed to Lucille L. Layton, Lady's maiden name. The return address is a medical clinic. I put it in Lady's underwear drawer, covering it with faded pastel panties and bras with stretched-out elastic. The next day my stomachache is better and I go to school. I never tell Duke. And I never ask Lady.

Sterling hung up the phone, then picked it up again and told Rosemary to hold any other calls.

"Did you ask Ryan if Rachel was with them?" I asked him.

"Probably not in so many words. We asked if he'd seen his sister walk away, if he'd seen anyone near her, if he'd seen anyone take her, if he'd seen anyone following them. I doubt that we ever asked him flat out if she was with them. He definitely never said she wasn't."

"Did he tell you she was a ghost?"

Sterling gazed up at the ceiling, looking back into the past. "Yeah, he did. 'Rachel's a ghost, she's invisible.' He said it several times. It was—"

"Spooky."

He didn't agree. But he didn't disagree, either.

"I need to make another phone call. Listen in again, okay?"

He heaved a sigh or two but he went back into Rosemary's office. I told the secretary at the high school it was urgent, I absolutely had to talk to Tony Fenton even if he was in class. "It's two-thirty," she said. "School just got out. I'll ring his room."

When he answered, I said, "This is Lizbet Lange. I have to know something."

"What?" He sounded impatient, almost angry. "I told you I don't know anything. I don't really remember much about it."

"Rachel was invisible, wasn't she?"

He didn't say anything for a long time, but I could hear him breathing. When he spoke, his voice was faint, faraway. "She was a ghost. I don't . . . I can't . . ."

"You tried to tell your mother, didn't you? But she didn't understand."

"I don't remember. I don't remember." He was whispering now. "I was four years old. For god's sake, I was just barely four years old."

"Tony? You never saw her, did you?"

"She was . . . she was there."

"But she was invisible."

". . . Ghosts are invisible. You can't see a ghost." He sounded mechanical, like he was repeating something he'd learned by rote, and never really understood. I was looking right at Sterling and I saw the shock, and the comprehension, in his eyes.

"I'm sorry," I said to Tony, "but I had to know."

"Yes," he said, and hung up. I had the feeling I'd just ruined the rest of his life. I didn't realize I was crying until Sterling handed me a tissue.

I patted the tears off my cheeks, telling Sterling that Holly Wood was going to come to the police department the next day. He already knew. Holly was his break in the case. When he was told she'd made an appointment he assumed she'd remembered something and he'd wanted to talk to her right away, but her husband was out of town for a couple days and she wouldn't talk to the police until he could be with her.

"She's been a basket case ever since she saw the billboard. She's going to tell you the same thing: Rachel was a ghost, Rachel was invisible."

"Rachel wasn't there." Sterling sat down heavily in his chair. He looked pale, like someone had just hit him in the stomach. "I remember . . . I asked Ryan if he remembered when he saw his sister last. I was trying to figure out the time element. He said . . . what did he say? He said something like 'I didn't see her. You can't see a ghost.' And he laughed. I thought he was just . . . I hadn't been around him much. He was a strange kid. He was hyper, couldn't sit still, couldn't seem to concentrate. I didn't think anything about it, I just thought he didn't understand. His sister was missing, his parents were frantic, cops were coming and going, there was a whole lot of commotion. I didn't think he really understood what was going on."

"There's another picture. Alicia Fenton has it. You should

take a look at it." I described it for him: four little trick-or-treaters and the boy behind them in his skeleton suit and his skull mask, his arm around his invisible sister.

"It was Brenda. It had to be Brenda. If she didn't kill Rachel, then Brad Hatcher did and she helped him get away with it. But I don't think she'd do that. If he murdered Rachel, I think she'd turn him in—if she didn't kill him first—even if he was her brother. I think she murdered her own daughter. The kidnapping was all a coverup. She had to have a ghost costume, a witch costume wouldn't work. She sent Ryan over to Alicia Fenton's with the sheet. *Ryan,* not Rachel. She'd already marked the eyeholes and the hem; she probably measured it on Ryan; they had to be about the same size. She picked a fight with Lucinda so there wouldn't be anyone with her except the four little kids and Ryan. And then . . . and then she told the children that Rachel was there but they couldn't see her because she was a ghost and ghosts are invisible. She must have told them over and over. They were so young. Ryan, well, he'd do what his mother said. I think he at least half believed it anyway."

Sterling was looking at the picture again, looking at Rachel, a little girl smiling for the camera, holding out the skirt of her long black dress with one hand, clutching a witch's broom in the other, a tall, pointed black hat on her head. A happy little witch, not a girl who would pitch a fit because she wanted to be a ghost.

"If you're right . . . If Rachel was already dead . . . it changes everything." He put the photo down again. "But . . ."

"But what?"

"But this picture isn't evidence of a crime. Let me tell you what will happen if you're right and I ask Brenda about it. She'll say, yes, Rachel had a witch costume; yes, she wore it for a picture. She'll say Rachel decided she didn't like the costume. She'll say she threw a temper tantrum. She'll say she told Alicia Fenton the costume didn't fit because she didn't want her to know that Rachel was being bratty. And the rest of her story will stay the same: Rachel went trick-or-treating with her. We can't prove she's lying, and after all these years of keeping it secret I don't think Ryan will change his story. Tony Fenton and Holly Brown—Holly Wood—they were four years old, small children traumatized by a kidnapping. They're useless as witnesses."

"But they're grown up now."

"Yeah, they're adults who suddenly remember that when they were four years old Rachel Wright was invisible. A lawyer would have a lot of fun with that, not that it would ever make it to court."

"Brenda's a wreck. Maybe she'd break down and tell the truth."

"I still can't believe that a woman who just killed her daughter could come up with a scheme like that."

"Brad Hatcher must have helped her. That's why he was killed. He was going to tell."

"After all these years? He'd implicate himself, and he'd have less chance of getting off than Brenda. She'd use an insanity defense. There are plenty of people who would swear she's been crazy for years."

"Well, maybe he didn't know back then, maybe he just figured it out and he was going to tell."

"That leaves Brenda coming up with the plan on her own, hiding the body, taking it to the field later. Handling her dead daughter's decomposing body. Besides, Hatcher was home all day. She couldn't have done it without him knowing."

"Didn't he work?"

"Midnight shift. Okay, he was probably asleep most of the day. Still, I can't believe she could do it."

"And Larry was definitely at work."

"Yes. No question about that."

"Well . . ."

"Where'd you get the picture? From Brenda's house, right? You went to see her again."

I nodded.

"She's the only one you talked to today who didn't call me up right away and tell me. How'd you manage to get it?"

I told him about the Barbie doll. He actually looked a little impressed. *"Girl sleuth,"* Charlie said, smiling down at me.

"Woman sleuth," I said, and he laughed. I had to bite the inside of my cheek to keep from laughing myself, that's how good his laugh is. You just want to laugh with him.

CHAPTER TWENTY-SEVEN

Sterling was going to try to talk to Holly Wood right away, instead of waiting until morning. I needed to get to my class so I couldn't wait around to see if he got hold of her, but he said he'd call me at home later and let me know what happened.

When I pulled into the high school parking lot, Jonathan was there, leaning against the front fender of his car, ankles crossed, thumbs hooked in the pockets of his jeans, looking almost as sexy as his father.

I pulled my car in next to his and he opened the door for me, kissing my nose when I got out.

"I was worried. I got to your place an hour ago. No note, no message on my voice mail, no nothing. Why's your cell phone turned off?"

I dropped my car keys into my purse and hitched the strap up on my shoulder. "Did you testify?"

"Yeah; two days sitting in a courtroom, thirty minutes on the stand."

"Did you do good?"

He grinned. "Nailed his ass to the wall. It'll go to the jury tomorrow. Not that it has anything to do with why your phone was turned off. What have you been doing all day?"

"I need to get to class, it's almost three."

"I'll walk you." He took my hand as we headed across the parking lot to the front of the school. "What have you been doing all day?"

Cops are so damn persistent. "Nothing much. I talked to a teacher and his mother this morning, had a drink at Jacob's with a woman named Holly Wood, went to the library, did my homework, read your e-mail, paid almost two hundred dollars for a Barbie doll, gave it away, stole a photograph, went to see Sterling, and solved Rachel Wright's murder."

We had stopped walking, not because I wanted to but because Jonathan had stopped dead, then swung around to face me, and even though I put my hand on his chest and pushed, he didn't move. He's a real immovable object when he wants to be.

He studied my face carefully, then said, "You read my e-mail?"

I laughed. "Sometimes I think I love you, Jonathan."

"Sometimes I think I love you, too. Look, I'm going to go to the store—somebody keeps forgetting to do the grocery shopping—but I'll meet you here when your class is out and I'll follow you home and we'll have a long talk."

"About your e-mail?"

"About your profligate ways. Two hundred bucks for a *doll?*"

Profligate. I'd have to look that one up. Although I could figure it out from the context.

I glanced at my watch. "I'm late." I tipped my face up for a kiss, then he said, "Run," and let go of my hand. I didn't run, but I did walk fast, with Charlie taking long strides beside me. The teacher was already droning on about factors when I slid into my desk. Charlie took the seat beside me, saying, *"My son seems like a good person."*

"The best. Now be quiet or I'll miss all this fascinating stuff."

The first half of class almost put me to sleep. At break time I walked around outside for a few minutes then went back to the room. The teacher was at his desk and looked up as I walked in.

"I drove past the billboard this morning," he said. "They've added information about a reward. I assume that's your doing?"

"Oh, that's good. I haven't seen it. My lawyer said he'd take care of it."

"I was talking to Fred Blanchard earlier today. He's retiring at the end of the school year. He's taught here since nineteen seventy-two."

There didn't seem to be anything to say to that so I just nodded. I mean, I didn't even *know* the man. Why would I care if he retired or not?

"He remembers Ryan Wright. Have you met him?"

"Ryan? Yeah, I have."

"How's he doing?"

I wasn't sure what he meant. "Well, he's all grown up."

He smiled. "I meant, is he living independently, supporting himself, that kind of thing."

"Oh. Well, he has a job at a warehouse. He lives with his parents."

He nodded. "They usually aren't able to live independently."

They? They who? Brothers of murdered little girls? Sons of cops? People with alliterative first and last names? "What do you mean? He had learning problems, I know. I guess he was hyperactive."

"He was almost out of high school before he was diagnosed, not that there's much a school can do. A structured environment helps, but life isn't very structured."

"Attention Deficit Hyperactivity Disorder, right? Some of the kids I went to school with had it. They had to go to the office to take their medication. He was an FLK, that's what someone who knew him said. A Funny Looking Kid."

"Hyperactivity can be a symptom, but his problem wasn't ADHD; it was FAS."

"FAS?" FLK, ADHD, FAS. The Wrights and the Todds should have thought of some of those letters when they were naming their kids.

"Fetal Alcohol Syndrome. I had a girl with it in one of my classes last year; it's very difficult to deal with."

"FAS. I guess I've heard of it but I don't know much about it."

"They're born with obvious facial anomalies: flattened face, flat bridge of the nose, no . . . I forget what it's called. This thing." He was using the tip of his little finger to rub the vertical groove above the middle of his upper lip. I didn't know what it was called either. I never even thought about it having a name. I realized I was stroking my own whatever-it-is and put my hand down quickly. "The physical differences are less noticeable the older they get."

"So you mean his mother drank while she was pregnant."

"Like a fish, I would assume. The babies sometimes smell like booze when they're born. Like they've been pickled in alcohol."

I made a solemn silent vow never to take even one little drink if I ever even thought about getting pregnant. "God, his mother must have been horrified when she found out. I mean, it was her fault, wasn't it? He would have been normal if she hadn't been drinking, right?"

"Right, although she probably knew, or at least suspected,

what was wrong with him long before an official diagnosis was made. The syndrome was recognized in the mid-'seventies, but that doesn't mean doctors didn't know about it before that. I'm sure obstetricians saw enough FAS babies to at least suspect there was a cause-and-effect relationship between alcoholic mothers and 'funny looking kids.'"

"Rachel was born less than a year after Ryan. She was okay."

"Her mother must have stayed on the wagon."

I listened to the racket from the babysitting room: a baby wailing, the wheedling voice of a babysitter trying to get someone to *please stop doing that*, a toddler crying *Mine! Mine!* over and over. I thought that having two babies close together might drive anyone to drink.

The teacher said, "She was probably a heavy drinker before, though. Most mothers of FAS kids have a long history of alcoholism."

"She would have only been in her early twenties when Ryan was born. She couldn't have been drinking for too many years."

"We have kids here who were alcoholics before they hit puberty. Usually their parents are alcoholics, too. That's where they get the liquor at first, from their parents."

Some of the kids I hung around with in high school kept bottles in their backpacks. I never thought of them as alcoholics. I guess I thought of them as cool.

My classmates were straggling into the room. After everyone settled down, Mr. GED Teacher started in on punctuation. I tried to pay attention but it's hard to get really excited about semicolons, you know? Charlie was sitting with his legs stretched out, hands linked behind his head, and before long I was working on a fantasy.

I hurried out of the building as soon as class ended, not

wanting the teacher to mention that I seemed to be miles away again. Charlie had smiled at me every time I glanced at him, which made me wonder if he heard what I was thinking. If he had, I'm surprised he wasn't blushing. Maybe ghosts can't blush.

I felt *myself* blush when I ran into Jonathan in the hall. As he put his arm around my shoulders and gave me a quick hug, I wondered if I was committing some kind of supernatural adultery. Not that we're married, but you know what I mean. I was cheating on him in my mind. With his *father.*

My classmates seemed to find Jonathan interesting, especially a couple guys who looked like they robbed convenience stores when they weren't in GED class. Jonathan had a holster on his belt and no one missed it. The women checked out his gun first, then the rest of him.

We let the others get ahead of us, then walked slowly down the hall, holding hands. Jonathan said, "I dropped by the police department."

"I thought you probably would. What did Sterling say?"

"He told me your theory."

"And?"

"It makes a lot of sense. In fact, screwing up the time-of-death estimate is such an obvious explanation for the delay in dumping the body that I'm surprised no one gave it more thought." Jonathan moved toward the wall, which was a solid row of lockers. He leaned his back against one of them and put his hands on my waist, pulling me against him. "Public displays of affection are forbidden in here," he said. "You want to break a few rules? We could sneak into a classroom and—"

"For pete's sake, Jonathan! My teacher's likely to show up any minute. He was still in the classroom."

"I don't think you're getting into the spirit of this," he said, his body moving slowly against mine.

"We'll get arrested."

"Cops don't arrest lovers," he said, nuzzling my neck, giving me goosebumps and warm tingly feelings. "We just tell them to get a motel room."

I backed away from him. "We'll be home in just a few minutes."

He sighed. "What's happened to your sense of adventure?" He smiled slowly. "Remember the hotel balcony in Hawaii?"

I remembered it. There were no teachers around and his father wasn't watching us. Besides, it was the middle of the night.

I yanked on his hand. "Let's go home. What else did Sterling say?"

He sighed again, but started walking with me down the hall. "He said he did consider the possibility that the killer wanted to make it hard to establish the time of death, but he ended up believing it was because of the search parties. Everyone believed the mother's story, so when the M.E. came up with a time of death that matched the facts—the facts according to the mother—he didn't see how the killer would benefit by delaying the autopsy. He figured the body was stashed somewhere in a hurry but had to be moved because eventually it would be discovered and the location would lead them directly to the killer. But there were people trampling all over the place for at least the first forty-eight hours after she disappeared, so he waited a few days."

"What did he say about her body being left where it was so easy to find?"

"He said if she was killed by some psycho, he left her where the voices told him to. But he's always believed the uncle did it. What was his name? Hatcher, right?"

"Brad Hatcher."

We'd reached the entrance. Jonathan opened the door and held it for me. As it closed behind us, he said, "And he figured Hatcher probably thought it would be better if the body was found. Until then, the possibility existed that Rachel was a runaway."

"She was only ten."

"They run at ten; it's not unusual. Sterling figured Hatcher wouldn't want them looking for a reason why she'd take off. Someone might have started thinking about the timing, wondering if her disappearance had something to do with the fact that her uncle moved in a few weeks earlier."

"Brenda killed her. Brenda wanted the body to be found so her husband wouldn't have to deal with never knowing if she was dead or alive. She probably didn't like the idea of Rachel rotting in the woods, either. He thinks I'm right, right?"

"He seems to think you've got the right idea, but he has a little trouble with the mother functioning well enough to come up with what you have to admit is an incredibly clever plan. I couldn't think that clearly if I'd just murdered someone, especially if it was my own kid. There's also the problem of motive. Why would she do it? The method doesn't really fit either. When parents go ballistic, it's usually obvious the kid was battered to death. Rachel was killed by a single blow to the back of the neck with some kind of metal rod, a jack handle or something similar."

"I didn't know that, not what it was."

"I don't think it was common knowledge. They might

have used the murder weapon as a way to weed out the fake confessions."

When we reached the cars, I said, "You can drive the Porsche if you want. I'll take yours."

"Okay, but it's not the same."

"The same as what?"

"Public displays of affection."

"Well, it'll just have to do until we get home. Rev it up a lot."

He laughed and slid into the driver's seat of the Porsche. I got into his car. He gunned the Porsche's engine and was out of the parking lot and way down the road before I even got his Chevy in gear.

The radio was tuned to a basketball game. I listened for a couple minutes then changed it to a rock station. Duke was a big sports fan. Hearing the game made me lonesome for him.

Nineteen seventy-three's the year they adopted the designated hitter rule, Duke says.

What's that?

Baseball, he says, which doesn't explain much. *The Oakland A's and the New York Mets went to the World Series in 'seventy-three. The A's won, four to three.*

That was the year of the Battle of the Sexes, Lady says, and Duke says, *Hunh! Tennis! Sissy game.*

This woman named Billie Jean King was a really good tennis player, Lizbet. She won at Wimbledon. That's like the World Series of tennis. She also played against a man named Bobby Riggs in a game they called the Battle of the Sexes. We won. Lady is smiling, smirking almost.

She was a lesbian, Duke says, and Lady says, *What does that have to do with it?*

I try to think of a question in a hurry because I have a pretty good idea what "battle of the sexes" means. It's fought all the time in our house.

What about football? I ask. Duke loves football.

The Super Bowl . . . 'Seventy-three was Super Bowl Seven. Miami Dolphins beat the Washington Redskins fourteen to seven at Rice Stadium. What else happened in 'seventy-three? He takes a quick hit off his joint. *I know: OJ—that's OJ Simpson, Lizzie-m'Lou—OJ was a running back for the Buffalo Bills and he broke Jim Brown's season rushing record from nineteen sixty-three. He set a new record—two thousand and three yards in one season. 'Seventy-three's when they started the World Football League with ten teams, but it didn't last long, only until 'seventy-five.*

They had stupid team names, Lady says. *The Philadelphia Bells, the Chicago Fire.*

Yeah, stupid names, Duke says, and I'm so surprised they agree about something that I ask another football question, but Lady ruins it by saying something about the AFL-CIO endorsing the Equal Rights Amendment in nineteen seventy-three, and Duke starts in about Women's Lib. Next to Watergate, it's the longest story I know, and it makes Duke even madder.

I turned the radio up louder, drowning out my memories.

CHAPTER TWENTY-EIGHT

I put Jonathan to sleep as soon as we got home, after telling Charlie to kindly go away for a while. He came back five minutes after I left the bedroom. His timing is amazingly good most of the time. So is Jonathan's, and it bothered me that after Charlie left I was going to forget why I really made that crack about bad timing. "I'm going to spend the rest of my life thinking I was stupid enough to say that, Charlie. Why did you have to show up then?"

"Sometimes my timing really does suck," he said, and laughed and made me laugh. Oh, well, it isn't like it's the stupidest thing I've ever done.

We sat in the kitchen, eating chips and dip and talking about the case. It was hard to picture Brenda killing her daughter then being cool enough to come up with a clever coverup, not to mention being cold enough to move her daughter's body three days after she died.

"Okay," Charlie said. *"If not Brenda, who?"*

"Brad Hatcher. But Brenda wouldn't have gone along with it, not if she knew he did it, and she had to know or why else would she claim Rachel went trick-or-treating?"

"Ruling out Hatcher leaves Larry Wright."

"He was at work. Besides, I just don't think he could do it."

"You've just ruled out all the possibilities. Who's left?"

"No one."

Jonathan woke up hungry about eight. We ordered a pizza and ate it in the casual living room while we watched a movie, one Jonathan wanted to see, with lots of big guns and explosions, but that's okay, he also watches the sappy movies I pick out.

Charlie was sitting in the armchair beside the couch, smiling every now and then at the two of us snuggled together on the couch. It occurred to me that if he hadn't died I never would have met Jonathan. I thought about that movie again— *It's a Wonderful Life*, with Jimmy Stewart. Jimmy Stewart wished he'd never been born and an angel appeared to show him how different things would have been if he got his wish. It wasn't Charlie's birth but his death that had changed things. And every time he came back, more things changed. I wondered how it could ever end. *Ramifications* is one of my vocabulary words. He was back because of the ramifications of his death, but couldn't his ghostly visits also have endless ramifications? Every time he shows up, things change.

After the movie ended, Jonathan wanted to check his e-mail, so we went into the library. I watched him play around on his newsgroups for a while, which is really boring, then he went to take a shower. He left the web browser on the screen so I went to a search engine and typed in FETAL ALCOHOL SYN-DROME. I got a list of a zillion web sites. The first one I looked at gave a list of symptoms, the ones Tony Fenton had mentioned and some others: microcephaly, which means a small head; small palpebral fissures, which are eye slits; epicanthal folds, which make the eyes of FAS kids sort of like the eyes of Down's syndrome kids; indistinct philtrum—that's the groove above the upper lip. Now I knew a word my GED teacher didn't know. Flat nasal bridge; flattening of the mid-face; thin upper lip; small jaw. Most of the websites had at least one picture of an FAS baby. They might have been Ryan Wright in the pictures in Rachel's album.

The behavioral symptoms were listed,too: low IQ, inability to learn from experience, moodiness, unpredictability, volatile temper, hyperactivity, inability to focus, vulnerability to peer influence, impulsivity, need for immediate gratification, inability to accept responsibility, lack of consideration for other people, cheating, lying, stealing, detachment about the trouble they get into, inability to understand cause and effect, inability to understand the consequences of their behavior.

"Those poor children, Charlie." I read the last line again: inability to understand the consequences of their behavior. I clicked on another link and read about a case in which a man with FAS killed a family. His mother said he knew he did it, but didn't really *understand* that he did it. Detachment from the problems they create.

I clicked on another link: a lawyer explaining that lots of people on death row are probably victims of FAS or FAE, which is Fetal Alcohol Effects, sort of a milder case without the physical differences but with the same behavior problems.

I was starting to get a weak, quivery feeling in my stomach. I clicked on another link: a report saying that maybe as many as half of all juvenile offenders have FAS or FAE.

Another link: the criminal justice system is based on the assumption that people understand why we have rules and why they have to be followed, but FAS victims don't seem to understand that. They don't understand that they've done something bad.

Another link: most FAS victims have poor reading and spelling skills, few are able to live independently, more than half run into trouble with the law, half end up having treatment for mental health problems, most have bad school experiences, dropping out or being expelled.

I clicked, clicked, clicked. The same words kept showing up: impulsive, volatile, detached, unable to understand cause and effect, unable to comprehend the consequences of their behavior, unable to comprehend the consequences of their behavior, unable to understand the consequences of their behavior. I minimized the screen, not wanting to see those words again.

Charlie was standing behind me. I swiveled the chair and looked up at him, my eyes burning with tears. "It was Ryan, wasn't it? That's how Brenda could do it. She was protecting her son."

"I think so. Talk silently; Jonathan may come back."

"The baby, too? Sudden Infant Death Syndrome. What if it wasn't? Remember what Lucinda told us? After Rebecca was born Brenda never slept. The other baby had died, so she watched Rebecca all the time. Then school started and Ryan was gone and she relaxed and she slept while he was at school. She was keeping Rebecca safe, wasn't she? Safe from Ryan. He hit Rachel and she died and his mother fixed it so no one would know. She'd already covered for him once."

"He wouldn't really understand that he was the cause of his sister's death."

"The consequences of his behavior. Oh, Charlie. Poor Brenda. No wonder she's half-crazy."

"She's to blame."

"Yes, but I bet she didn't understand the consequences of her behavior either, not when she was pregnant and drinking. They have all those warnings now, but I don't think they did back then. I don't think women knew drinking could hurt their babies. She must have been so sad when she realized what she had done to him, how she had changed him forever before he was born."

I heard a tiny click from the computer behind me and knew

the screensaver had come on and tiny stars were flying to the edge of the screen and disappearing, an unchanging, unending stream of stars, going nowhere, but going there constantly.

"She's spent her life protecting him," Charlie said.

"From the consequences of his behavior. Poor Brenda. God, poor Larry. Do you suppose he knows? Would she have told him?"

"I doubt it. My impression is that he honestly doesn't know what happened to Rachel."

"Mine, too. No, I don't think she told him. I think it's her secret. Do I have to tell Sterling? Maybe it would be better if no one ever knows."

"People need to know the truth. That's why I'm here. I think it might have something to do with Rebecca."

"Rebecca? Rachel and Ryan's little sister? I never even met her."

"She just had a baby, remember? Maybe it's that baby we're protecting. Rebecca doesn't know she needs to be careful when Ryan's around the baby. He's her brother, her baby's uncle. She would trust him. But I don't think he can be trusted around children. He had three sisters; two of them are dead. Now he has a niece."

"He's in his thirties. He must have been around children lots of times."

"But not left alone with them. Brenda would have seen to that. Besides, no one would have left their kids with him. He's too strange, too much a child himself in many ways."

"But Rebecca might."

"Sure. He's her big brother. She has no reason to think he would ever hurt anyone. Brenda has kept Ryan's secret for all these years. I don't think she would break her silence now. She'd convince herself that Ryan wouldn't hurt Rebecca's child. She'd probably try to make sure he didn't have the chance, but he isn't a child anymore, she can't watch him every second. Once the truth about Rachel's death is known, the baby will be protected from Ryan. And Ryan will be protected from himself."

"Poor Ryan. He was the first victim."

"Yes. And because of you, Rachel will be the last."

CHAPTER TWENTY-NINE

Before we went to bed, I told Jonathan what I'd found out about Fetal Alcohol Syndrome and what I thought had happened to Rachel. He held me close until I fell asleep and in the morning he called Sterling for me and told him about the consequences of Ryan Wright's behavior.

I was a little surprised that Sterling believed it right away. But it made sense. It solved the last mystery: it explained how Brenda Wright could come up with a devious plan to conceal a murder. She could do it because she was protecting her child. Sterling hadn't talked to the Wrights yet; he said he needed to figure out how to approach them because he had no evidence, and definitely no grounds for an arrest. He had talked to Holly Wood, but couldn't make an arrest based on her childhood memories. It was after Jonathan hung up that I remembered there was one mystery left. We still didn't know for sure who killed Brad Hatcher. Well, Sterling would just have to figure it out himself. I was finished.

Jonathan spent the morning with me. He had to work the first four hours of his shift in the afternoon, then another cop was filling in for him in the evening so he could be at my party. I wasn't really in a party mood, but I didn't have any choice since it was my party.

The Party Hearty people showed up in the afternoon, right after Jonathan left. They removed the rugs from the formal living room so we'd have hardwood floors for dancing, took out some of the furniture to make more space, and set up a portable stage for the band. Then they hung spider webs made of fine silvery thread all over the downstairs. I'd told them I wanted something tasteful—no skeletons or coffins or tombstones—but I wished now that I hadn't agreed to spider webs, even if they did go with my costume. It made me think about my dream, about being caught in a giant spider web, trapped in Charlie's web.

At five the caterers showed up. At seven I went upstairs and showered, then put on my costume. I decided not to wear the face mask because it made me feel too warm, and claustrophobic. I put on black slingback heels, but before I went downstairs I changed into the soft leather boots from Jill's Jeans 'n Things. My spider legs were floating at my sides. They were going to take some getting used to.

The party was sort of a blur when I thought about it afterward, probably because I had two tequila sunrises right after I greeted the first guests at the door.

Mrs. Altman apologized for not being "fashionably late." She was wearing a beautiful brocade gown and a huge white wig. I thought she was Martha Washington but she said she was Dolly Madison. Her husband looked like George Washington but I suppose he was Dolly's husband. I looked past them and almost groaned out loud.

Coming up the walk was a motorcycle cop named Jason Johnson and his girlfriend, Tiffany. Jason shaves his head and has muscles I didn't even know existed, and which no one was going to miss tonight because he was naked except for an oversized diaper. Against the white of the diaper, his skin looked almost black. Tiffany was dressed in a leopard skin and had bronze glitter all over her bronze skin, and that was a whole lot of glitter because most of her skin was visible. I shooed the Altmans inside and grabbed Jason's arm as he walked in the door. "If that diaper comes off, I'm going to make Jonathan arrest you."

Jason laughed so loud the walls shook, and Tiffany jumped on his chest and wrapped her legs around his waist, flashing the thong undies she was wearing beneath the leopard skin.

That's when I headed for the bar, leaving the door open so the rest of the guests could come on in. The bar was set up in the dining room where a ton of food was so beautifully arranged that it seemed a shame to touch it, let alone eat it. Black vases of orange flowers were placed among the platters of food, and the delicate silver spider webs were draped all over the place.

By the time my second tequila sunrise took effect, having four extra legs seemed perfectly normal to me, and the first floor of my house was filled with vampires and mummies and witches and aliens from outer space and Humphrey Bogart wannabes with hats pulled low over their eyes and trench coats belted tight and Marie Antoinettes and Abraham Lincolns and flappers and punk rockers and gangsters and gorillas and . . . no Jonathan.

I was getting ticked and thought I might just have another drink when I saw him coming in the front door, cleverly disguised in a dark blue San Jose Police Department patrolman's uniform. I hurried down the hall and said, "*Great* costume, Jonathan," very sarcastically.

"You look good enough to eat," he said, and gave me a quick kiss. "I caught a burglary in progress, had to stay and do the paperwork." He set the shopping bag he was carrying on the floor and pulled out a few miles of light tan cloth, which he tossed over his head, jamming his arms through sleeves, the fabric falling to the floor around him. He pulled his shoes and socks off, dropped them in the shopping bag, shoved his feet into sandals, then settled a turban-and-veil thing on his head. Lawrence of Arabia.

"Better?" he asked.

I grinned. "I've always had a thing for Peter O'Toole. But I picture him naked under his robe, not in a cop uniform."

"Peter O'Toole? Sexy? Peter *O'Toole?* You gotta be kidding." He stashed the shopping bag in the coat closet, then kissed me again. "Are we just a little tipsy?"

"We are not," I said, trying not to weave too much as we walked into the formal living room.

The band was between songs. I wasn't sure if the band members were in costume or if they always looked like that. Half my guests were talking about their stock portfolios and the other half were talking about drug busts and hot chases. Even if they'd all been talking about the weather it would have been easy to tell the two groups apart. My neighbors were the ones who knew some adjectives besides "fuckin'."

The band started playing a fast song. Jonathan had walked away to talk to someone, so I watched the dancers for a while, feeling a little dizzy as a pirate gyrated past with a pink rabbit, and a mummy dirty-danced with an M & M. Across the room, a rubber-faced Richard Nixon in a black suit and white shirt was listening to a talkative marine with streaks of green and black camouflage paint on his face and leaves stuck through the mesh on his helmet. I hoped the machine gun wasn't real.

Sherlock Holmes, who lived down the street from me and whose wife was around somewhere, was standing way too close to Tiffany. I looked around and spotted Jason coming in the room carrying two drinks. He stopped suddenly, staring across the crowded room at Sherlock, whose hand was now on Tiffany's waist. I took a good look at Jason's diaper as he walked across the room, trying to figure out if he was armed.

Jonathan's partner, Suzanne Wilkerson, appeared at my side, holding a plate piled high with hors d'oeuvres. "Did you have some of this shrimp stuff?" she asked.

I hadn't had anything at all to eat. I looked up at Suzanne, who is about six feet tall barefoot. She was wearing a long, slinky, gold lamé gown and gold shoes with four-inch heels, and she had big hair instead of her usual short, tight curls. "I think Jason's going to kill Sherlock Holmes. Who are you?"

"Suzanne. How drunk are you?"

"I know who you are, I meant your costume."

"Diana Ross, the Supreme. Lord, Jason really does have a gun in that diaper, doesn't he?"

"I think he's just excited because he thinks he's going to get to kick some butt. Oh, there you are," I said to Jonathan as he slid an arm around me and pulled me close, squashing my spider legs against my side. "Go stop Jason, will you?"

"Stop *Jason?* I don't have a death wish, sweetheart. You should have hired some security guards."

"The place is crawling with cops. Why would I pay for security guards?"

"Because the place is crawling with cops."

"Well, I didn't. Oh, good, Tiffany's got him under control."

Jonathan started picking hors d'oeuvres off Suzanne's plate and popping them into his mouth.

"That guy must have cleaned out his garage," Suzanne said.

"I haven't seen one of those rubber Nixon heads in years. Damn it, Dillon, go get your own food and leave mine alone."

The band started playing something fast with a good beat. "You want to dance?" I asked Jonathan.

"I want to eat."

I wanted to dance. *"You want to dance with me?"* I asked Charlie. He smiled and said, *"Why not?"*

I found an empty corner and started dancing, by myself to anyone who was watching, but really with Charlie. Charlie danced like Duke and Lady danced, 'sixties-style. I followed his lead, my spider legs bouncing along beneath my arms.

When the song ended, an Abraham Lincoln I recognized as the CEO from down the road came to a clumsy halt in front of his clown partner and smiled at me. "Can't find a partner?" he asked. "That's hard to believe."

"I'm dancing with Charlie," I told him. "He's a ghost."

The CEO looked at the empty space in front of me and said, *"Great* costume!"

A slow song started. I was tempted, really I was, and Charlie was smiling, but I just couldn't make myself touch him. Besides, no one was drunk enough to deal with the hostess slow-dancing in the arms of a ghost.

Jonathan was suddenly at my side, saying, "Isn't that our song they're playing?"

I put my hand in his, and stepped close. "I didn't know we had one."

"They're all our songs," he murmured into my ear, sending shivers up my spine.

A little after eleven I heard the doorbell and hurried to the entry, wondering who on earth was showing up so late. Chief

Sterling was standing on my doorstep, dressed in his usual gray suit.

"What are you supposed to be?"

"A party crasher. Thought I'd stop by and see how the rich folks live."

"I told you you could come. Come on in. Don't arrest anyone."

"I'm off duty."

"The bar's in the dining room," I said, pointing the way. Later, I came across him sound asleep in a recliner in the casual living room. He looked kind of sweet asleep, not like a cop at all.

The music played, the dancers spun, the food disappeared, the liquor flowed. Suzanne fell in love with a bank president and asked me if I thought an interracial relationship would work. I looked at her new love, who had shiny green reptile skin. "That would be interspecies, wouldn't it?" I asked and Suzanne choked on her soda and lime.

About one in the morning, I was standing in the living room watching Jonathan dance with a pretty flapper. After the song ended, I chatted with the woman for a few minutes, complimenting her rose garden, which borders my property. She rattled on and on about aphids and blight. The third time she called me Lizabeth, I slapped my forehead with the palm of my hand. Jonathan and Charlie both raised their eyebrows, looking like those two peas in a pod. A champagne cork popped in the dining room and the flapper said, "Oooh, I love that sound," and headed for the bar. I grabbed Jonathan's hand. "We have to talk to Sterling."

"Now? It's pretty late."

"He's here."

"He is?"

"He's sleeping. Come on."

"Sleeping?"

I tugged on his hand and headed for the casual living room, where Sterling was snoring in the recliner, an empty wine glass held loosely in one hand. I shook him awake, saying, "Come with me. It's important."

Sterling and Jonathan—and Charlie, of course—followed me to the library. I leaned against the edge of the desk, facing them. "People misunderstand my name all the time," I said. "Lizbet isn't very common and people get it wrong. Some of them think I'm saying Lizbeth because some homeless guy wrote a book about a dog that was named Lizbeth—it was on the bestseller list or something—or they think I'm saying Lizabeth because there was an actress named Lizabeth Scott who was in a movie with Humphrey Bogart. I don't remember the name of it. I've never seen it. Duke told me about it. But anyway, people know Lizbet's short for Elizabeth, but no one thinks I *say* Elizabeth when I tell them my name because . . . I guess because they know I didn't say that long a word and they know that whatever I said started with an L, so they guess Lizbeth or Lizabeth because they've never heard Lizbet before."

Jonathan and Sterling were both looking at me like they'd just read *Men Are From Mars, Women Are From Venus* and knew they weren't supposed to say *For chrissake, get to the point.*

Charlie, bless his ghostly heart, said, *"Put them out of their misery."*

"My car registration has Elizabeth Ann Lange on it."

Jonathan got it first. "Who called you Elizabeth?"

"Luther Todd."

Sterling looked stunned. "He was my sergeant back then. He was . . ."

"Leading the investigation?"

"More or less . . . Alicia Fenton was right. I knew he was seeing Brenda. They were lovers for years. Hell, everyone knew. Everyone but Larry and Lucinda, I guess. Luther's dying, liver cancer." He sighed, then said, "I'll talk to him, but it's too late tonight. He's sick. I'm not going to wake him up. He isn't going anywhere. It'll wait 'til morning." He adjusted his tie, smoothed his lapels. "I think I'll go home. Great party, Ms. Lange. Good wine."

"And a comfortable recliner," I said and he smiled, just a little. We walked to the front door with him and told him goodbye. Jonathan and I were heading back to the dance floor, when Charlie said, *"We need to talk."* I told Jonathan I was going to the bathroom, and that, no, I didn't need any help, thanks anyway.

Charlie and I went upstairs to my bedroom. I sat on the edge of the bed, standing up again quickly when Charlie said, *"I have to leave now."*

"No! What do you mean? You can't leave. It isn't over yet."

"Shhh. Jonathan might follow you up. It is over, Lizbet. Todd killed Brad Hatcher. Ryan killed Rachel. That's it. You did good."

"But, Charlie . . . I don't want you to go."

"I know, but I have to. You'll forget me in a few days, but you'll still have Jonathan."

I nodded. *"Your son."*

"Yes. The only part of me that's real." Charlie smiled at me, that heartbreaker of a smile. *"Close your eyes,"* he said. *"No peeking."*

I closed my eyes. When I opened them again, he was gone. I couldn't go downstairs right away. I didn't cry, I wouldn't let myself cry. I just sat on the bed, all my spider legs motionless beside me, learning the full meaning of one of my vocabulary words: bereft.

The party wasn't the same with Charlie gone. I just wanted it to end. It was two in the morning when the guests started leaving. I helped Jonathan match up the drinkers with their designated drivers, and then stood by the door, listening to everyone gush about the party and tell me I should do this again soon. I didn't think I would.

After a while I realized Jonathan had disappeared, and I wondered if he was on the Internet, or naked in bed. Naked in bed, I hoped, but, if not, I thought I could get him away from his newsgroups by telling him I needed help getting out of my costume. A few minutes later, I heard the pop of a champagne cork from somewhere upstairs and smiled to myself. We could drink it in bed.

By two-thirty I was alone in the entry. I locked the door, turned on the alarm, yawned, moved my arms up and down a few times to watch my spider legs move, then walked through the downstairs, picking up a few stray glasses. The caterers had cleaned up the kitchen and dining room before they left and the Party Hearty people would come back tomorrow afternoon to clear away the decorations. I was so tired I was almost hoping Jonathan was asleep, or too involved in the Internet to notice me.

I was almost to the stairs when I heard a noise behind me and turned around, expecting to see Jonathan. I jumped about a foot when I saw Richard Nixon instead, fifteen feet from me by the door to the casual living room.

"You scared me," I said. "The party's over. Do you need a taxi?"

He didn't answer. He raised his hand from his side and I realized that was a gun he was pointing at me.

CHAPTER THIRTY

My first thought was: a cop. One of Jonathan's friends, with too many drinks in him and a warped sense of humor. Please, a cop, a drunk, a friend. But I'd talked to all the cops and none of them was Richard Nixon.

My second thought was: a *cop!* How stupid we'd all been! They were *all* cops, and a cop is a cop forever. Even a retired cop could find out where I lived without much trouble and the catering van and the Party Hearty truck were parked out front all day, practically screaming *Halloween party! Come on in! Come in costume—nobody will know who you are.*

My third thought was: a killer. And that sickening "uh-oh" feeling in my stomach meant I was right. A killer, here to shoot me with that gun with the long tube on its barrel. Semiautomatic, I thought; you can't put a silencer on a revolver. Semiautomatic, like Jonathan's Glock.

Jonathan.

My voice came out at least an octave too high: "Where's Jonathan?"

"I know they had you wired," Richard Nixon said in Luther Todd's voice. He took a step toward me. I took a step back.

"Wired? What are you talking about?"

"I saw you talking into your wire in the car when you left my place. Forgot I was still there, didn't you? But I didn't give anything away. What's the matter, they wouldn't take your word for it that it was me you saw?"

"I wasn't wired. I was talking to Charlie."

If a rubber face can look confused, he looked confused.

"He's . . . he's, like, an invisible friend."

"At your age?"

"Where's Jonathan?"

"Is that your boyfriend? I got rid of him."

"Got rid of him?" The words rattled around in my head until I made a connection: champagne cork popping upstairs; silencer. My heart stopped, started, beat raggedly. I took a step toward him. He took a step back. "You *shot* him?"

"Don't come any closer," he said, shoving the gun toward me a little.

"You shot Jonathan? You shot *Jonathan?!*" My voice went shrieky, out of control. Horrible things were happening inside me, my insides were knotting, jerking, aching. I spun around and ran down the hall toward the stairs, shrieking Jonathan's name.

"Hey! Stop!" I heard him moving behind me, coming after me. I kept running, one part of my mind waiting for the gunshot that would be the last thing I ever heard, another part totally insane with anger and fear.

"Jonathan!" I leapt up to the fourth step and took the rest three at a time, spider legs flailing all over the place, ripping loose from their Velcro tabs, dangling from my wrists, tripping me. I fell, banging my shin hard against the riser, but I was up again before I had time to feel the pain and I reached the top of the stairs just as I heard Luther start up them.

He fired as I darted into the first bedroom; I screamed and

slammed and locked the door, so scared I thought I'd been shot because I couldn't get a breath after my scream. The room was so dark after the brightly lit hall that I felt blinded for a moment, uncertain of my bearings, then I made out the shape of a long dresser against the wall, not far from the hinged side of the door. I was trying to shove it toward the door when he jerked on the doorknob, then started throwing himself against the door. The dresser wouldn't slide on the carpet. I lifted the end of it and swung it around in an arc so the front was against the door. It only covered half the door but it was heavy and it would slow him down. I scrambled across the bed, losing three of my legs on the way, and grabbed the phone on the night stand, punching nine-one-one then dropping the receiver on the bed. I'd just remembered that this room had a shared bathroom, with a second door that opened into the next bedroom, and that room's door would be standing open. I almost slammed the bathroom door but caught it and closed it quietly, realizing too late that of course it didn't lock from the bedroom side. I jerked it open again, ran across the bathroom—why are all the bathrooms so *big!*—and closed and locked the other door. There was nothing in the bathroom to shove against the door to the next room, nothing to use as a weapon, nothing but guest soap and towels. No hair spray, no shaving cream, nothing I could spray in his face. I ran back into the bedroom and grabbed the chair from in front of the dressing table and jammed the back of it beneath the bathroom doorknob.

Luther was panting out obscenities between blows to the door. The lock had broken and the door was banging repeatedly into the dresser. I looked around frantically for a weapon while some deranged part of my mind was calmly planning to stockpile them—a loaded gun in every room, grenades, a cannon.

There was nothing in this room but furniture and linens and pretty little bedside lamps that weren't heavy enough to hurt anyone. I was vaguely aware that I was panting *please god, please god, please god* over and over. My last spider leg was dangling from my wrist. I ripped it off, snapping the fine plastic thread.

The dresser slid an inch or two forward; Luther's fingers curved around the edge of the door. I thought of the gun, thought of a bullet coming through the door, but I couldn't let him get in, I'd die for sure. I ran to the dresser and yanked a drawer out of it, one of the three small top drawers, and swung it like a baseball bat, smashing his fingers. He yelped in pain and then the door was banging into the dresser again, pounding it back inch by inch, as his shoulder slammed again and again into the door. I scrambled up on top of the dresser and stood up, holding the small drawer in both hands, facing the ever-widening opening, aware of sirens outside, close but not here yet.

The dresser jerked each time he slammed into the door. It was like skateboarding on cracked asphalt, the dresser moving in little hitching bounces. I had to lean one way then the other to counterbalance myself and I still almost slid off each time it moved, and it was moving, moving, moving. When I thought the opening was big enough for him to squeeze through, I lifted the drawer over my head, holding it by the sides, the front with the big brass handle facing down, and when his head and shoulders appeared in the opening I brought the drawer down as hard as I could on top of his head, the impact jarring my wrists and shoulders so hard they went numb and I dropped the drawer and a gun fired once, twice, a third time. I lost my balance and fell off the dresser, landing hard on my knees. I looked down at my front, expecting to see blood spurting out of me, but there wasn't any, then I heard a *thump* from the hall and Luther Todd was sliding downward in the opening, his upper body held upright in the narrow space, then slumping over onto the bedroom floor. The sirens were right outside now, and someone was knocking down my front door. The alarm suddenly whooped, the sound so loud it hurt, then just as suddenly it stopped.

I got to my feet, shaking, staring at the rubber head with a jagged rip in it, blood seeping through. I wondered where Luther's gun was, but he was so still I wasn't too worried about it.

It was quiet downstairs. I thought they must be inside the house, sneaking around, not sure what was going on, whispering into their radios, asking the dispatcher if he could hear anything; all the pounding and screaming and gunfire would have been heard through the phone on the bed. I thought I should call out to them, but I couldn't seem to get enough breath. I realized I could hear Luther breathing harshly, sounding far away, then his voice, raspy, whispery, saying "Honey . . . honey . . ."

Honey?

"Jonathan!?"

I squeezed through the opening, stepping all over Luther Todd, and fell to my knees beside Jonathan, who was flat on his back against the wall, tangled in his Lawrence of Arabia robe, turban half off, gun still in his hand, eyes closed, face deathly pale. At the center of his chest was a hole surrounded by burnt fabric. I screamed *"Get an ambulance!"* then *"Code Thirty! Code Thirty!"*—magic words, *cop in trouble,* nothing makes them move faster, and someone downstairs called out something I didn't understand. I had my hand on Jonathan's chest and could feel it rising and falling and I could hear his breath wheezing in and out, but he was so pale, so very pale.

"It's safe!" I shouted, "but get an ambulance, Jonathan's hurt!" A deep voice said something, then two Oak Valley cops appeared on the stairs, just head and shoulders first, coming up with their backs against the wall, guns drawn. They holstered them when they reached the top and saw Luther Todd's legs sticking out of the bedroom, and Jonathan so quiet, and me with tears streaming down my face, and they knew that whatever it was, it was over.

Chapter Thirty-one

Brenda Wright would have taken her secrets to her grave if Luther Todd hadn't blabbed on the way to his. Sterling let me listen to the tape recordings of his interviews with them.

Four years before Rachel died, little RuthAnn Wright was smothered in her crib by her big brother, who only wanted to make her stop crying. "He didn't understand what he did," Brenda said over and over. "He didn't understand that she was dead because of what he'd done. I couldn't tell anyone. How could I tell anyone? He's my son."

She kept that secret until the day when, sick with grief and frantic with fear, she called her lover to ask for help because Ryan once again didn't understand what he'd done, *couldn't* understand because his mother drank her way through her first pregnancy.

Larry and Brenda had both been heavy drinkers, starting in high school. "Lots of pregnant women drank," she told Sterling, her voice surprisingly calm. "No one told us not to. When he was born, when Ryan was born, the doctor looked at me, this look of total disgust. 'Your baby was born drunk,' he said, 'born drunk and brain damaged.' That was all. He didn't help, he didn't tell me what to do. He'd never told me not to drink. Why didn't he tell me not to drink? I didn't know I could hurt my baby, no one told me." She never had another drink after Ryan was born, after the doctor told her what she'd done to her child.

On Halloween afternoon in 1973, Rachel and Ryan were in the garage, cleaning the seeds out of pumpkins so they could make jack-o'-lanterns. Rachel got upset because Ryan threw a glob of seeds on her. They were gooey, slimy, and she started crying. "He can't stand it when people cry, even now," Brenda said. "Crying bothers him. He just couldn't stand it." Brenda went in the house to get a washcloth to clean Rachel up so she'd stop crying, but Ryan stopped her before his mother got back.

"She was on the floor, so quiet, so quiet. I asked Ryan what he did. 'She was crying, Mama,' he said, 'I made her stop crying.' She was . . . so still, so quiet. I touched her. I knew she was dead. I didn't know what to do. I called Luther. He didn't want to help me, he said I had to tell, but how could I tell anyone? Ryan didn't understand what he'd done. I told Luther . . . I told Luther I'd tell Lucinda about us if he didn't help me. He was mad, he was so mad, but he did it. He took her away, he took Rachel away."

The fake kidnapping was Luther's idea. He wanted Brenda to call all the parents and tell them she couldn't take their kids out trick-or-treating, but she thought that would seem funny. "I thought of the ghost costume, that was my idea. I just got rid of Lucinda and her kids. The other ones, they were so young it was easy. I took the ghost costume with me in Rachel's trick-or-treat bag, and I made Ryan put it on in the restroom in the park. Don't talk, I told him, don't say a word, and I told the little ones he was Rachel, I told them it was Rachel in the ghost costume, and when Ryan took it off a little later I told them they couldn't see Rachel anymore because she was a ghost. Rachel's a ghost, she's invisible, that's what I told them. They were so young. It was all mixed up in their heads, they wouldn't make any sense if they tried to tell anyone. And Luther made sure none of the cops questioned them too much."

Sterling's voice said: "She was wearing the costume when her body was found."

"I gave it to Luther. He put it on her before he . . . before he moved her. I don't know where she was. I didn't want to know. An empty house, he said. The people were on vacation, he was watching the house for them while they were gone. I told him he had to put her where she'd be found. I didn't want her in the woods, lying in the woods forever."

I don't really feel sorry for Brenda, even if she only did it to protect her son, but I sure feel sorry for poor Brad Hatcher, who Sterling thought was a child molester and a kidnapper and a killer, but who never did anything but keep his mouth shut when he should have talked.

I think he must have been a pretty good cop. He was asleep upstairs Halloween afternoon, until Brenda woke him up to watch the baby. He never knew what was going on downstairs but he figured it out later from little things: his sister's nervousness; her insistence that she couldn't wait until Larry got home to go trick-or-treating; the way she sent him upstairs to get the baby's pacifier and then left the house right away, calling up the stairs to tell him they were going trick-or-treating. It was after he was asked to take a lie detector test that he read all the reports, knowing he was a suspect and remembering those little things, and remembering that he'd never actually seen Rachel on Halloween afternoon. It was the autopsy report that clinched it for him. He knew his sister would never give her kids a sandwich and chips for dinner.

He confronted Brenda and she broke down and told him

the truth. She was his sister. He didn't tell. He kept her secret for years, and he might have kept it forever if the billboard hadn't made him feel guilty, and if his niece Rebecca hadn't told him how nervous Ryan got when he was at her house and her new baby wouldn't stop crying. Brad told his sister he had kept quiet too long, that people needed to know what Ryan was capable of doing. Brenda told Luther and they confronted Brad in his rental house while Lucinda was out for the evening.

"I couldn't talk any sense into him," Brenda said. "He was going to tell. We left the house and we sat in my car for a while. Luther was furious, furious at me for what I made him do when Rachel died, and furious at Brad because he was going to tell. 'Never a blemish on my record,' he kept saying, 'and now this is going to come out and that's what I'll be remembered for.' He told me to wait and he went back to the house. Brad opened the door for him, then I saw him trying to close it but Luther pushed his way in. I thought I heard a shot, I wasn't sure. Luther came out, he stopped by the car window and told me to turn off the dome light, then he walked over to Brad's other house, the one across the street; I didn't know why until he got in the car and told me."

Luther had been standing close to Brad when he shot him and was splashed with blood. He didn't want to let Brenda leave until he was sure she would keep quiet about Brad, so he used the outdoor faucet at the house across the street to wash the blood off. He was going to go back to his own house after he told Brenda to go home, but he saw me and decided it would be better if they both left in the car. He had blood on his shirt that hadn't washed off, and didn't want the shirt in his house in case the police suspected him. They were only a few blocks away when Brenda remembered there was an old sweatshirt of her husband's in the trunk, so Luther changed into it and left the bloody shirt with Brenda to throw away. She dropped him off around the corner from his house and he went in the back door, then walked out front, acting like he was curious to see what all the cops were doing at the house next door. They all knew him; no one suspected him of anything. He told them he'd been sleeping, that his medication made him drowsy and he hadn't heard a thing. Everything had gone his way; no one had come outside to investigate the gunshot, the cops hadn't shown up too soon. "It would have worked," Brenda said. "No one would have ever known. But *she* saw him."

That was me: *She*.

Luther didn't tell Brenda exactly what happened in the house, but he told Sterling that Brad threatened him with the gun, and he got it away from him and fired in self-defense. Sterling doesn't believe it because there was no sign of a struggle. Brad's wife said he always kept the gun handy when he was working alone in one of his rentals, and Sterling thinks Luther saw it when he was in the house with Brenda and he went back deliberately to kill Brad. I guess it doesn't really matter, since Luther's dead now.

Sterling doesn't know what will happen to Brenda, or to Ryan. Or to Larry, who never knew what was going on, but he did lie to the cops and tell them Brenda was home when her brother was killed. "I just told him it would be easier," Brenda said. "We already knew what it was like to be suspects; we'd been through that with Rachel. I told him I didn't want to go through it again. He thought I was at the cemetery, visiting Rachel. I do that a lot."

The only mystery left—besides how Ryan could bear to live with a mother who cries non-stop—is why Luther didn't shoot me the way he shot Jonathan, without warning, without a word. He blew his chance to get away with Brad Hatcher's murder by letting me know who he was. After he talked to me it was too late, too late to change his mind about killing me and too late to run when he heard the cops coming. But I guess he thought I'd already identified him as the man I saw on 13th Street and he was mad that I'd botched everything up for him, and I suppose he thought if he was going to get caught for one murder, he might as well make it two. After all, he didn't have to worry about going to jail; the doctors said he only had a couple months left.

Sterling thinks he didn't shoot me right away because I'm a woman, that it was harder for him to shoot a woman than a man. He thinks he needed to work himself up to it and he didn't have enough time. But I think it might be because he had met me; he knew me, at least a little, but Jonathan was just a faceless stranger in a dark room. Nothing personal, just *Bang!*

Luther only lived for two days, although the doctors said he would have survived both the gunshot and the knock on the head if he hadn't been so weakened by cancer. I don't think Jonathan and I will feel too guilty about it. I was defending myself and Jonathan thought he was saving my life, although I think I did that myself. Jonathan only hit Luther once and that was in the thigh; his other two shots went into the wall beyond the foot of the stairs.

My house was a mess. The front door was broken off its hinges and they smashed the wall by the alarm box and ripped out wires and there was blood all over the carpet upstairs and that door was ruined and so was the door frame, and Jonathan hit the wall in my bedroom when he was shot and cracked the plasterboard. And there were the bullet holes, of course. But it's all been fixed, and you'd never know it ever happened. Some things are easy when you're rich.

Some things aren't. I've been staying at Jonathan's apartment, with his temporary roommate snoring in the next room all night. I just don't want to be at home, not by myself. Maybe it'll be better when Jonathan gets out of the hospital tomorrow. He has a concussion and he has cracked ribs; his chest is so bruised I can't bear to look at it.

I rode in the ambulance with him and he was conscious for a while. "I was going to take it off," he told me. "I was going to take my uniform off, I was going to give you your Peter O'Toole fantasy. If he'd been just a little slower . . . I was going to take it off."

I put my hand on his shoulder, feeling his body armor. I leaned down close to him. "Don't you ever take it off," I said, my voice all weak and shaky.

"I won't," he said. "Not around you, anyway," and he laughed and it must have hurt because he passed out. He'll be fine though. He's already fussing about missing work. I bought him a laptop computer to play with at the hospital and that perked him up a lot.

Chief Sterling paid my parking tickets.

I still remember Charlie but my memory of him is fading away. I just think of him every now and then. I still know he was here, but pretty soon I won't. Mostly I remember him leaving, I remember him smiling, saying, *"Close your eyes. No peeking."*

I did close my eyes and I didn't peek and I didn't feel a thing, but somehow I knew I'd just been kissed a ghostly goodbye. And I heard what he whispered as he left: *"Until next time."*